THE SOCIAL ENGINEERING OCCULT

THE SOCIAL ENGINEERING OCCULT

Revealing the
Masters of Delusion

Axel Pétur Axelsson

CONTENTS

FOREWORD

In the intricate dance of society, where shadows play upon the walls of perception, there exists a manuscript steeped in an enigma, its origins as elusive as the morning mist that cloaks an ancient forest. This manuscript, a relic of a time untethered to the known authors of history, beckons the curious and the brave to peer into its depths.

Crafted with the meticulousness of a time-forged masterpiece, it navigates the hidden mechanisms of influence and control, those silent puppet strings that orchestrate the grand masquerade of civilization. Readers are invited on a journey through veiled truths and hushed schemes into the heart of the subtle manipulations that have shaped the narratives of existence from behind a curtain of obscurity.

With each page turn, revelations unfurl, echoing the wisdom of lost epochs. They resonate through the corridors of time, from the whispered secrets of antiquity to the pervasive streams of our digital agora. The narrative speaks with a voice that transcends the ages, rich with the echoes of ancient myths and brimming with contemporary allegories.

This exploration stands as a tribute to the relentless human pursuit of knowledge, a pursuit that sails the vast ocean of what is seen and dips into the undercurrents of what is not. It is an odyssey that seeks to illuminate the artful dance of reality, where every truth holds hands with illusion.

As readers embark on this formidable journey, they may find themselves equipped with new lenses to observe the world. The unveiled secrets and reflective insights contained within these pages are an invitation to become more discerning, more aware, and ultimately more adept at navigating the nuanced interplay of hidden forces that shape our collective experience.

In the grand tapestry of society, this manuscript serves as a hidden thread, guiding those who follow it toward a deeper understanding of the unseen artisans of consensus and the silent choreographers of public thought. Let this not just be an introduction but a call to the awakening—a revelation of the most profound puppetry, crafting reality's grand narrative from the shadows of forgotten lore. Welcome to the threshold of the most incredible show unseen, where the past whispers to the present, and the foundations of the world are laid bare for those who dare to look.

CHAPTER 1

In the realm of governance, one must push aside the veil of eloquence to scrutinize the essence of each notion. Through astute comparison and logical inference, illumination is cast upon the tapestry of reality that envelops us.

Our discourse now unfolds to reveal our orchestrated schema from dual perspectives—that of the enlightened and that of the uninitiated masses. Recognizing that those driven by base instincts outnumber the virtuous is essential. History has shown that the reins of the masses are best held through determination and awe rather than the futile endeavours of scholarly debate. Ambition is the universal creed; all covet a throne, and few are those who would not barter the collective good to ascend to personal glory.

What chains have held back the predatory instincts inherent in humankind? By what means have the unruly been shepherded through the annals of civilization? Initially, they were tamed by the unyielding might of unseeing force; subsequently, by Law—a transformation of that very force, yet cloaked in guile. Thus, the inexorable Law of nature decrees that might is the precursor of right.

The notion of political liberty is no more than a spectre, an illusion. Yet, this spectre is to be wielded deftly when it serves to trap the multitude in pursuit of a cause, to topple those in seats of power. This endeavour finds its ease when the adversary has been seduced by the very same ghost of liberty, the so-called liberalism, and is prepared to forfeit a measure of sovereignty for its ideals. Herein lies the pinnacle of our stratagem; the loosened grip on the reins of rule is promptly clasped by hands anew, ready to steer. For the unguided force of the nation falters even briefly without a master, and so, seamlessly, the new order slips into the vacated mantle of the old, now frayed by the ideals of liberalism.

Gold's Dominance and Its Unseen Influence

In the epoch where we stand, the dominion of liberal sovereigns has been supplanted by the dominion of Gold. There was an era when Faith reigned supreme, yet now the concept of freedom proves elusive, for its judicious use escapes the grasp of all. When the reins of governance are handed to the populace, chaos ensues, transforming the collective into a dishevelled throng. Such disarray begets strife, tearing the fabric of society asunder until the once-mighty states crumble into insignificance, their very essence reduced to cinders.

Whether consumed by its internal tumults or weakened by discord that invites foreign dominion, a state finds itself irreversibly ensnared within our influence. The tyranny of Capital, over which we exert unwavering control, extends a deceptive lifeline to the beleaguered state—a choice between salvation and oblivion, though both paths lead inevitably to our threshold.

To those of liberal persuasion who might decry these tactics as devoid of morality, consider this: if a state, beset by enemies, may justly employ all strategies in conflict against an outward adversary, can it not similarly employ such strategies against a more insidious foe—one that corrodes societal pillars from within? Can one genuinely expect to guide the masses with reasoned discourse when even the most illogical dissent finds favour among those who wield reason as a mere veneer?

In the realm of politics, morality plays no role. A ruler swayed by a moral compass needs to be equipped for the chessboard of governance, for political mastery demands guile and the art of illusion. Those virtues held dear by the masses—honesty and integrity—are but liabilities in the political theatre, capable of dethroning monarchs more effectively than any adversary. These are the hallmarks of the Public's domain, not ours, for our path is one of pragmatism and dominion.

The Rule of the Powerful

In the intricate dance of power, our dominion is anchored not in the ethereal concept of "right" but in the tangible, inexorable might of force. "Right" is but a nebulous construct, a spectre evoked to justify the pursuit of desires. It stands as a testament to strength, a proclamation that one's power overshadows another.

Where, then, do the boundaries of "right" lie? They stretch only as far as the reach of power, vanishing into the void where weakness begins. Amidst the labyrinthine structures of governance, where authority has been diluted, and laws have become but shadows of their intent, we perceive a new "right"— the prerogative of the mighty to dismantle and rebuild, to sweep away the vestiges of a crumbling order and erect a bastion over those who have surrendered their sway to the seductive illusion of liberalism.

Our power, veiled from sight, grows ever more formidable amidst the decay of traditional rule, its unseen roots spreading deep and wide until it stands unassailable, impervious to the machinations of the cunning. From the ashes of momentary turmoil, a new order will arise, steadfast and enduring, steering the gears of society back to a path defined by order, not by the caprices of liberalism. In our grand design, we weigh not the scales of morality against utility but focus on the difficulties of necessity.

Before us lies a grand strategy, a path so meticulously charted that to stray but a hair's breadth could spell the doom of epochs of labour. To sculpt a plan of action that bears fruit, one must account for the unpredictable nature of the mob—its fickleness, its volatility, and its blindness to the intricate web of its existence. A mob is but a leviathan of blind force, ever susceptible to the merest whisper of suggestion.

Only those nurtured in the cradle of sovereignty, schooled in the intricate tongue of politics, can truly grasp the reins of leadership. The masses left to their own devices, spiral into chaos, torn asunder by internal strife over power and prestige. Can such a disparate crowd, devoid of personal stakes, forge judgments, withstand adversaries, or safeguard the realm? It is a notion as absurd as it is futile, for a collective without unity is no more effective than a symphony without a conductor, a cacophony doomed to fade into silence.

Thus, we stand vigilant, the unseen architects, orchestrating the future with a lexicon of power known only to those destined to rule.

The Architects of Silent Supremacy

Within the grand tapestry of governance, the threads of power can only be woven by a singular, despotic hand, orchestrating the vast apparatus of state with precision and clarity. Such is the only governance under which civilization, that delicate creation not of the masses but of the visionary, can truly flourish. The crowd of humanity, left unchecked, is but a beast of savagery, poised to descend into chaos at freedom's untutored grasp, a chaos that is the very zenith of barbarism.

Consider the hedonistic thrall in which the masses entangle themselves, a right to excess that is misguidedly equated with freedom. It is different from the path of those who hold the reins of power. The youth, intoxicated by the libations of liberalism and seduced by the siren call of early depravity, are guided there by the very hands supposed to mould their virtue—by educators and caretakers, by those entrusted with their care in the opulent halls of the wealthy, and even by the glittering society dames who lead the charge in the halls of decadence.

Our watchword is unyielding—Force married to Illusion. Only the hidden strength that wields the quill and sword with equal finesse can truly hold dominion in the shadow play of politics. Governments must not falter or lay their sceptres down before the spectres of new ideologies without a fight. In the theatre of power, we do not shy away from the cloak and dagger of deception, for in its embrace lies the path to our ultimate goal.

Our state strides forward on a path paved not with the clamour of war but with the silent march of a more insidious conquest. One way a state can maintain control is by replacing the spectacle of battle with a subtler orchestration of terror, which ensures blind allegiance from its subjects. The creed of the state is founded upon an austere and unyielding might that does not hesitate to dispense with mercy in the pursuit of its loftiest aim—total dominion. This doctrine of unrelenting force will ensure our victory and the capitulation of all sovereignties beneath the omnipotent shadow of our supreme governance. All must understand that our resolve is unbreakable, our retribution unflinching, and from this recognition, all dissent will wither.

Liberty Shall Cease

In the dawn of days, our voices were the first to weave through the crowds of the masses the enchanting mantra of "Liberty, Equality, Fraternity" – a spellbinding trio of words that, ever since, have been parroted by the unseeing, drawn inexorably to the allure of these ideals, which once ensured the safeguarding of individual sovereignty against the crush of the collective.

The so-called sages of the populace, those intellectuals, grappled in vain with these ethereal concepts, blind to the truth that equality and freedom are illusions in the grand design of nature. Nature has ordained a tapestry of minds, characters, and abilities as diverse as the stars and decreed an order as unyielding as her own eternal laws. The rabble, in its blindness, elevates its own from the mire to rulership, heedless of the fact that true adeptness in governance comes not from widespread acclaim but from the cryptic depths of political acumen—a knowledge guarded within the sanctum of dynasty, a sacred flame passed from sovereign to heir, invisible to the governed and invulnerable to the passage of time.

As the wheel of time turned, the essence of dynastic stewardship over the hidden machinations of politics began to fade from the collective consciousness, fortuitously cementing the ascendancy of our cause. Across the globe, the heralds of "Liberty, Equality, Fraternity," unwittingly enlisted by our unseen agents, carried our banners high with fervour, unknowingly ingesting the seeds of discord that would erode the tranquillity, unity, and bedrock of their nations.

This subversion laid the groundwork for our greatest triumph, allowing us to seize the ultimate lever of control—the dissolution of the ancient and noble hierarchies that once shielded the realms from our influence. Upon the ashes of this ancestral aristocracy, we erected a new order—an aristocracy of enlightenment and wealth, each tier held firmly within our grasp, each echelon driven by the engine of knowledge bestowed by our venerable elders.

The deft manipulation of human frailty facilitated our conquest—the lure of wealth, the hunger for material satisfaction—each failing alone enough to quell the spirit of defiance and bind the will of men to our dominion. The mirage of autonomy we spun led the collective to believe their governance was no more than a caretaker of the people's will, a caretaker that could be readily replaced should the fabric of their service fray.

This idea of interchangeable leadership puts the power in our hands, allowing us to control the fate of nations from the shadows with a mere whisper. This power was once unimaginable but is now ours to keep.

CHAPTER 2

In an era where the very fabric of war is interwoven with the threads of economic gain, it is crucial to our dominion that such conflicts do not extend their reach into territorial conquests. Wars must be strategically directed to the economic arena, where the nation's eyes will be opened to our influence's subtle yet overwhelming force. In this new battlefield, the vulnerable states will inevitably find themselves reliant upon our expansive international network—a behemoth of surveillance and influence, unrestrained by any earthly law. Our global dominance will eclipse the concept of national sovereignty, asserting our supremacy with the same ease that a nation's laws command the actions of its citizens.

The bureaucrats, handpicked from among the populace for their unerring submission, will be unversed in the intricate ballet of governance, rendering them mere instruments in our grand symphony. They will be deftly manipulated by the actual puppeteers—our scholarly elite, who have been meticulously groomed since the cradle to orchestrate the grand narrative of world affairs. Our erudite advisors, privy to the most guarded secrets of statecraft, draw from our reservoir of political stratagems, the wisdom of history, and the ceaseless tide of current events.

The masses, guided not by the rational application of historical insight but by the seductive allure of theoretical dogma, will remain oblivious to the intricate web we weave. They are content to bask in the illusions we have conjured, their beliefs shaped by the very science they revere—a science that our thought architects have deftly manipulated to mould their perceptions as we see fit. The intellectuals of the masses, inflamed with their own so-called knowledge, will blindly champion these theories without scrutiny, unwittingly enacting the grand designs that our experts have subtly inscribed in the annals of their education.

The Erosion of Enlightenment

Consider not the following declarations as mere rhetoric but rather as a reflection upon our profound influence on the collective consciousness. Our strategic promotion of Darwinism, Marxism, and Nietzscheanism has not been without calculated intent. For those among the elite, it should be lucidly apparent how these doctrines have served to unravel the fabric of the Public's traditional beliefs and values.

Our mastery must meticulously appraise the intellectual and cultural currents, the distinct spirits and inclinations of the nations. Any oversight in the political domain or the governmental affairs orchestration could jeopardise our supremacy's intricate design. The success of our system, a complex engine with components that can be adeptly adjusted to resonate with the unique temperaments encountered along our journey, hinges on the astute assimilation of historical wisdom illuminated by contemporary reality.

In today's geopolitical theatre, a formidable force exists that shapes the zeitgeist, a force known as the Press. The Press's role is manifold: it incessantly highlights the essential demands, amplifies the populace's grievances, and fosters a sense of unrest. It embodies the pinnacle of free speech, a concept the Public

States have failed to exploit, thus allowing this power to slip stealthily into our grasp. It is through the Press that we exert our influence, cloaked in obscurity, and through the Press, we have hijacked the precious metal of gold despite the harrowing toll it has exacted in blood and sorrow. Yet this price has been met with acquiescence, for the losses we endure are an offering to a greater vision, where the fall of one of our own is outweighed by the downfall of a thousand of theirs in the divine calculus.

CHAPTER 3

In this twilight of epochs, we stand upon the threshold of dominion, with only a sliver of the void left to bridge. The grand odyssey we embarked upon is on the cusp of completion, heralded by the closing embrace of the Symbolic Serpent, our clandestine emblem. As this cycle concludes, the nations of Europe will find themselves trapped within its spiralling grasp, clutched by an unyielding force.

The constitutional mechanisms of the modern era are poised to crumble, crafted by our design with an intrinsic imbalance, destined to perpetually waver until they erode the very fulcrum of their rotation. The masses labour under the delusion of their fortitude, constantly awaiting the moment of equilibrium. Yet, the monarchs, ensconced upon their thrones, are besieged by their delegates, the jesters of governance, overwhelmed by the magnitude of their unbridled and unchecked sovereignty. This dominion, born from the shadows we've cast within the corridors of power, renders these rulers impotent, unable to bridge the chasm separating them from their subjects, diminishing their strength to counter the usurpers of their authority. We have orchestrated a chasm between the sovereign's perspicacious jurisdiction and the populace's oblivious might, rendering each impuissant in isolation, much like a sightless man bereft of his guiding staff.

We have sown discord to provoke the power-hungry into the reckless exercise of might, setting every conceivable force at odds and dismantling their natural inclinations towards autonomy. In our machinations, we have provoked every form of ambition and equipped all factions, transforming governance into a coliseum of chaos. A touch more, and the unrest of insolvency shall be ubiquitous.

The garrulous have transformed legislative assemblies and councils into battlegrounds of rhetoric. The audacious press and the unscrupulous pamphleteers besiege officials with relentless critique. The crescendo of misused power will lay the final groundwork for total subversion. As all structures quiver on the brink of collapse, they shall be hurled into the heavens by the frenzied upheaval of the masses, now untethered and tempestuous.

Poverty as a Tactic

In the age of machines and mythos, the common man finds himself bound in the invisible chains of necessity more securely than by the irons of old servitude. Where once serfdom and slavery held sway, a new yoke has been wrought from the adamant of poverty—a bond from which escape seems but a siren's song. The charters of liberty we have woven into the very fabric of the state offer rights to the masses—ethereal and illusory figments of freedom that, in the harsh light of day, reveal their ghostly countenance.

For the labourer, whose silhouette is bent in ceaseless toil, the dreams of liberation are but whispers drowned by the cacophony of his reality. The grand discourse of liberty, the freedom of speech that lets orators spin their grandiloquent visions, the freedom of the press that permits the quill to dance across the page, unfettered and frenzied—these are but mirages to the weary spirit whose daily bread is earned in sweat and dust.

The rights claimed to be given to the people are nothing but illusions in the bigger picture of governance. It is a cruel joke played on those who are at the mercy of those in power. They are left with mere scraps from the table of the privileged and wealthy. Their only role in this grand design is to cast their lot with the figures we place upon the stage of power, mere puppets to our unseen hand.

The notion of republican freedom serves as a bitter jest to the impoverished soul, for whom the relentless pursuit of sustenance leaves no room for the fruits of such freedom. Instead, it strips him of the promise of a steady hearth, placing him at the mercy of the tumultuous tides of his brethren's unrest and the caprices of those who rule the anvils and the looms.

Advocating for Collective Solutions

Under our subtle dominion, the masses have razed the nobility to the ground, the very guardians who were their shield and nurturing matrons, all for a perceived self-gain entwined inseparably with their prosperity. With the fall of nobility, they have tumbled into the clutches of relentless magnates, who have imposed an iron and heartless yoke upon them, grinding them down without respite.

We emerge as the heralded liberators of the toiling masses, extending an invitation to join our ranks—the vanguards of socialism, anarchism, communism—always under the guise of brotherhood and the universal fraternity of our clandestine brotherhood. Once the lawful benefactors of the workers' toil, the aristocracy had a vested interest in their sustenance and vigour. Our interest lies starkly opposed—we seek to diminish, to extinguish the populace. Our sway is rooted in perpetual scarcity and the ensuing frailty of the worker, making him a pawn to our designs, powerless to resist our dominion. Starvation confirms the dominion of wealth over labour with a certainty no royal decree could match.

From scarcity, envy, and malcontent, we shall incite the masses, and their own hands will clear our path of any obstacle. And when the time is ordained for our sovereign to ascend as the master of all, these very hands shall cast aside any remnant of obstruction.

The populace has been weaned off the faculty of independent thought, save for the promptings of our scholarly agents. Blind to the pressing need for the changes we will enact when our era dawns—a shift to instil in the national consciousness a solitary, vital truth, the bedrock of all understanding: the knowledge of the intricate tapestry of life and society that necessitates the division of labour, and thus the stratification of men into classes and stations.

It is crucial for all to grasp that due to divergent pursuits in human activity, equality is unattainable; one who jeopardizes an entire community cannot stand on equal footing before the law with one who merely tarnishes his own honour. A true insight into the framework of society—a mystery from which we exclude the masses—would reveal to all that roles and responsibilities must be confined within defined bounds, lest they become a font of misery borne of a mismatch between education and the tasks individuals are destined to fulfil.

With a profound understanding of this truth, the populace will willingly yield to governance, embracing the roles delineated for them within the state. Currently, marred by the direction we have steered their understanding and bolstered by a naive faith in the printed word, they harbour—a result of our carefully orchestrated misdirection and their ignorance—a blind hatred towards ranks they perceive as superior, utterly oblivious to the essence of class and condition.

Preservation of the Privileged

In a realm where power and myth intertwine, where the future is forged by the unseen masters of technology and ancient lore, a great upheaval is orchestrated from the shadows. A grand crisis of economy shall be conjured, using the clandestine alchemy of gold and subterranean machinations—all within our grasp—to unleash upon the European streets a tempest of labourers. Once occupied with toil, their hands will be compelled to seize what they have long coveted from those they've naively envied since birth.

Yet, this storm will not tarnish our own, for we shall have foreseen the moment of tumult and fortified ourselves against it. We have shown that the path of progress inevitably leads the masses to the throne of reason. Our reign, though despotic, will be one of enlightened severity, a beacon of order amidst chaos, expunging the wildfire of liberalism from the institutions it has sought to consume.

Like moths to a flame, the people, once drunk on the nectar of freedom, have stumbled and groped for guidance, only to lay their sovereign power at our feet. Recall the grandeur of the French Revolution—a spectacle crafted by our design—where the Public was led from disillusionment to disillusionment until they sought refuge in the embrace of the foretold monarch of divine lineage, whom we have groomed for them.

We are an unstoppable international force, bolstered by some nations even as others assail us. The Public's base nature, grovelling before might yet ruthless against weakness, has unwittingly hastened their own subjugation. They endure the iron fist of modern tyrants with a docility that belies their spirit, a spirit that would have once risen up against the slightest royal misstep.

What strange paradox is this, that the masses accept the whispers of their current dictators, believing in high-minded ideals of welfare, universal brotherhood, and equality, all the while blind to the truth that such unity can only be realized under the dominion of one sovereign rule?

And so, the masses absolve the guilty and condemn the innocent, growing ever more convinced of their omnipotence. Amidst this disorder, they dismantle the pillars of stability, waging war against all forms of authority, divine or natural. Thus, when our time comes to ascend the throne, the concept of 'freedom' must be purged, for it breeds only the savagery of beasts slaked temporarily by violence. These beasts would otherwise resist the chains of civilization.

CHAPTER 4

In the grand tapestry of republics, a narrative as ancient as the fabled labyrinth that confined the Minotaur, each nation inevitably weaves through the same cyclical saga. The infancy of such a republic is marked by a period of chaos—an era where the masses, blind as the seer Tiresias but lacking his divine foresight, surge and swell in a tumultuous frenzy, casting their fates to the winds in every direction. From this primordial tempest, the seed of demagogy takes root, flourishing into a wild garden of anarchy, which in turn ushers in the era of despotism. But this is not the despotism of old, ruled by a sceptre and crown, visible to all and thus accountable. No, this is the shadow rule, an empire of whispers and intrigue, far more potent for its invisibility.

Like a pantheon of old gods, this covert authority ensconces itself behind the veil of mortal affairs, and its omnipotence felt yet seldom traced to its source. It manoeuvres through intermediaries as ethereal and untouchable as the strings of fate, the ever-shifting agents and proxies that carry out its will, their disposability ensuring the longevity and inviolability of the power behind them. Continual change becomes the cloak under which this power thrives, for in the churning waters of political turnover, it finds its secrecy unchallenged and its existence unsuspected.

Who can lay siege to a citadel that breathes amid legend? Who can dismantle an influence as pervasive and intangible as the air of Olympus? Such is our force—akin to a modern myth, where the lodges of public masonry unwittingly serve as the bulwark for our clandestine dominion. The architecture of our power, its very sanctum, remains an enigma as unfathomable as the riddles of the Sphinx, shrouded in the mystery of the unknowable, protected by the shadows of a problem that the public, in its collective innocence, cannot begin to unravel.

Undoing the Sacred

In a world where freedom is as mercurial as the shifting sands of time, its essence could harmonize with the state's mechanisms, preserving the common weal if grounded in the bedrock of divine faith. Imagine a society buoyed by an unwavering belief in a celestial order, a brotherhood not anchored in the deceptive shallows of equality but in the profound depths of hierarchical harmony that the cosmos itself adheres to. In such a world, the populace would navigate life's labyrinth under the benevolent gaze of spiritual stewards, their souls aligned with the divine will manifest on Earth. Yet, it is imperative to unravel this tapestry of faith, to extract from the public's heart the threads of spirituality, replacing them with the cold, hard calculus of materialism.

To trap the minds of the public in the web of constant labour, their thoughts must be ever directed towards the ceaseless engine of commerce and industry. Thus absorbed, nations will sink into the mire of profit, blind to the looming spectre that unites against them. To ensure that the chalice of freedom becomes the poison that withers the communal spirit, we must set industry adrift on the volatile seas of speculation. What the land yields shall slip through grasping fingers into the voracious maw of our dominion.

This relentless pursuit of supremacy, the jolts to the heart of economic life, has already sown the seeds of communities bereft of warmth, empty of soul. Such communities, grown cold and indifferent, will eschew the lofty ideals of statecraft and faith, their compass fixed on acquiring wealth. Gold will ascend as their new deity, worshipped for the earthly paradise it promises. And when the moment is ripe, not in search of virtue or riches, but propelled by a hostility towards the elite, the proletariat will cast their lot with us, their new clandestine sovereigns, against the intellectuals who stand in our path, the unwitting heralds of an age they cannot foresee.

CHAPTER 5

In an age where the very fabric of society is interwoven with threads of corruption, where wealth is a trophy for the cunning, achieved not through honorable means but through the shadows of deceit, and where morality is upheld not by the intrinsic values of the heart but by the cold, unyielding grip of law, one must ponder the nature of governance that can shepherd such a flock. Amidst this maelstrom, where the sacred bonds to faith and fatherland are unraveled by the doctrines of a borderless world, the only governance that can stand is one of an iron-clad despotism, the likes of which shall be revealed.

Imagine a construct of power, a central force so potent, that it clasps every thread of the communal fabric within its unbreakable hold. Through the meticulous engineering of laws, every political pulse within our subjects' lives will be orchestrated, each freedom methodically rescinded, each indulgence systematically revoked. Thus, our reign will be heralded by a despotism so grand, so pervasive, that at any whisper of dissent, at any corner of existence, it shall possess the might to extinguish the flame of any Public opposition with but a breath.

Detractors may claim that such absolute rule is a relic, incompatible with the enlightened strides of our era, yet the annals of history are ripe with testament to its efficacy. In bygone eras, when the divine right of kings was as unassailable as the heavens, the masses bowed in silent reverence to the thrones' decreed fate. But once we planted the seeds of doubt, casting kings down from their celestial pedestals to the realm of mortals, and once we stripped away the veneer of divinity from both monarch and deity, the scepter of power was abandoned on the thoroughfares of the Public domain, only to be deftly claimed by us. In the ensuing void, we stand poised to forge an empire, cloaked not just in the vestments of temporal power, but in the unassailable armor of divinity usurped.

Untruths That Lead

In the grand tapestry of control, it is the unseen weavers who hold true dominance, their hands deftly spinning the narratives and doctrines that guide the unwary. Our mastery, derived from an ancient lineage of sagacity, lies in sculpting society with words and tenets so abstruse, so ensconced in their complexity, that the Public gazes upon them in bemused ignorance. Cultivated in the arts of keen analysis, observation, and the exquisite finesse of strategic foresight, our insight is unmatched, eclipsing all others save for the once-vaunted Jesuits. They, however, have been relegated to the annals of history by our design, presented to the masses as nothing more than a conspicuous institution, whilst we have remained shrouded in enigma, our conclave operating from the shadows.

For there may come a time when the forces of the world could converge against us, a coalition of the Public spanning across continents. But such unity is but a chimerical notion, for we have sown the seeds of discord so deep that they have taken root in the very core of nations. Personal vendettas, nationalistic zeal, religious schisms, and racial enmities have all been cultivated by our hands over the millennia, ensuring that no single state dared stand allied against us. In every clandestine negotiation, every whispered treaty, our influence is the silent yet omnipresent spectre.

It has been foretold that it is through our agency that monarchs rule, an affirmation proclaimed by prophets, that we, the chosen, are divinely mandated to govern the terrestrial sphere. Bestowed with prodigious intellect to fulfil this sacred duty, our adversaries, regardless of their ingenuity, find themselves pitted against an adversary of ancient might and profound rootedness. The battle, should they choose to engage, would be, without precedent, a clash of titan against fledgling, where the brilliance on their side is but a nascent glimmer against our enduring luminescence.

The engines of statecraft and dominion are driven by the relentless power of gold, a force that we command. Political economy, a discipline crafted by our enlightened elders, has long since anointed capital with regal authority. The wheels of governance across all lands turn to the rhythm set by this engine, and the engine of worldly machinery is fueled by the very gold that rests in our hands, the glittering cornerstone of our indomitable empire.

The Power of Economic Control

Capital, like the unbridled current of a mighty river, must flow unrestricted, carving pathways that lead to the consolidation of industry and commerce into the hands of the few. This is the silent transformation unfolding across the globe as if guided by the hand of an invisible architect. Such liberty in financial realms shall grant a herculean political clout to those who harness the gears of production, furthering the subjugation of the populace. In this modern epoch, it is paramount to disarm the people, not through warfare, but by harnessing their ignited passions for our gain rather than attempting to douse their fervent flames; it is paramount to guide their erasure.

The cornerstone of our directive stands thus: to sap the vitality of the Public's intellect through incessant critique, to veer it from contemplation that might spark a rebellion, to scatter their cognitive might into a charade of bombast and futile discourse.

Throughout history, the masses, like individuals, have mistaken rhetoric for action, satisfied with the mere illusion of progress while seldom scrutinizing the integrity of words against deeds. Therefore, we will erect grandiose institutions that perform an elaborate pantomime of societal benefit, a pageantry of progress.

We shall adopt the visage of all factions and ideologies, bestowing upon this façade a voice through orators who will saturate the air with their verbosity until the listeners' patience is worn thin and their tolerance for speechcraft turns to loathe.

To ensnare the public opinion firmly within our grasp, we must lead it into a bewildering maze by projecting a cacophony of conflicting viewpoints, prolonged until the Public loses its bearings, resigned to the belief that apathy is preferable to the labyrinthine complexities of political affairs, which are best navigated by those who steer the Public will. This is our primary hypothesis.

The secondary hypothesis vital to our governance's triumph is this: to increase societal shortcomings, habits, and passions to such a degree that confusion becomes the status quo, rendering mutual understanding impossible. This chaos will also serve to inflame discord across all factions, to disintegrate any collective resistance yet unyielding to our dominance, and to thwart personal initiative, which poses a peril greater than the indolent compliance of the disunited masses. Any spark of personal ambition, especially one driven by genius, could rival the machinations of an uncountable number who have been infused with discord by our hand. Education must thus be orchestrated so that upon facing a challenge requiring initiative, the Public will falter in helpless resignation.

The liberty of individual action drains vigour when it confronts the freedom of another, culminating in profound moral upheavals, disillusionments, and failures. Through these methods, we will exhaust the Public to such an extent that they will be compelled to extend to us an international authority, one that will incrementally absorb all worldly state powers and birth a Super-Government. A spectre will supplant the rulers of today, this Super-Government Administration, whose reach will extend like omnipresent pincers and whose organizational expanse will be of such monumental scale that it will invariably bring all the nations of the earth to heel under its omnipotent shadow.

CHAPTER 6

In the near future, we shall initiate the genesis of titanic monopolies, vast treasuries of immense wealth upon which the considerable fortunes of the masses will be so reliant that they shall sink alongside the crumbling credit of nations in the wake of political upheaval. Those amongst you, sages of economic lore, ponder the magnitude of such a confluence!

With every manoeuvre conceivable, we shall amplify the stature of our Super-Government, portraying it as the guardian and saviour to all who yield to its embrace. The political potency of the Public's nobility has been extinguished; they no longer merit our concern in governance matters. Yet, as landlords, they maintain a capacity for nuisance rooted in the self-reliant nature of their estates. It becomes imperative, then, that we strip them of their terra firma. To achieve this end, we shall encumber their lands with burdensome debts and obligations that landholding becomes not a symbol of autonomy but an anchor of servitude.

The highborn among the Public, intrinsically unsuited to a modest existence, will be swiftly consumed by their extravagance like stars expending their final energy destined to collapse into obscurity.

The Invisible Chains

We must fervently champion commerce and industry, prioritizing above all the arena of speculation, which serves as a balancing force against the tangibles of industry. The vacuum left by a speculative industry's absence would result in capital swelling in the coffers of private hands, inadvertently resurrecting agriculture by releasing the land from the clutches of crippling debt owed to financial institutions. Our design is that industry should siphon away labour and capital from pastoral lands and, through the alchemy of speculation, transpose all monetary wealth into our custody, thereby casting the entire populace into the proletariat's echelons. Subsequently, the masses will prostrate themselves before us, driven by the sheer necessity to secure a semblance of existence.

To hasten the demise of the Public's industrial prowess, we will harness the allure of luxury we have nurtured within them, that insatiable lust for luxury that devours all. We shall institute inflation of wages, which, paradoxically, will offer no reprieve to the workers as we simultaneously orchestrate a surge in the cost of essential commodities, citing this as the aftermath of a decline in agriculture and livestock production. Simultaneously, we will cunningly erode the very bedrock of production by luring workers into chaos and indulgence while strategically extinguishing the enlightened minds of the Public from the earth.

To ensure that the masses remain oblivious to the actuality of their predicament until the appointed time, we will don the guise of zealous advocates for the working class, shrouded in the rhetorical principles of political economy, around which our theoretical doctrines incessantly weave a persuasive narrative.

CHAPTER 7

The escalation of military might, and the proliferation of law enforcement are pivotal to the fruition of our grand design. Our vision is such that, across all the nations of the globe, there will exist, apart from ourselves, nothing but an ocean of the proletariat, interspersed with islands of millionaires allied to our cause and the guardians of order — the police and soldiers.

Across the expanse of Europe and through our tendrils extending into other continents by virtue of our European connections, we must be the architects of turmoil, strife, and hatred. This strategy bestows upon us a twofold boon. Firstly, we maintain a stranglehold over all nations, for they are well aware that at our behest, we can unleash chaos or bestow peace. These nations have grown to regard us as the omnipotent arbiters, the essential force capable of quelling the storms we conjure. Secondly, through our machinations, we shall entangle all the cords we have cast into the governmental sanctums of every state, entangling them with political and economic pacts and ensnaring obligations of debt. To achieve this, we must employ unparalleled shrewdness and insight in our negotiations and contracts, yet in matters of public discourse, and we will don the visage of integrity and amiability.

In this manner, the masses and the rulers of the Public, indoctrinated to judge only the surface of what we present before them, will continue to uphold us as the altruistic heralds and saviours of humankind.

Warfare as a Global Constant

We must hold power to quell any defiance with immediate and overpowering might, unleashing conflicts upon the neighbouring realms of any state that dares to challenge our authority. Should these neighbours unite against us in a rare front of solidarity, we will counter with the threat of a global conflict, a war of such scale and might, echoing the epic battles of lore, where gods and mortals clashed in the celestial arenas.

The linchpin of triumph in the intricate dance of politics lies in the enigmatic cloak of our manoeuvres: the utterances of our diplomats should never align with their covert actions. In the artful play of politics, as in the mythical schemes of old, it is the unseen hand that directs the fate of nations.

We shall manoeuvre the governments of the Public to act unwittingly as pawns in our grand strategy, which edges ever closer to its majestic finale. We shall craft the illusion of a Public will, a sentiment that seems to rise from the masses but is, in truth, a melody composed by us and played out by that omnipotent instrument — the Press. A press that, with negligible exceptions, already dances to our tune.

To encapsulate our method of maintaining the Public's governments within our sphere of influence in Europe, we shall exhibit our formidable might to them through chilling acts of terror. And to all, if we contemplate the eventuality of a universal rebellion against our dominion, we shall retaliate with the thunderous firepower of distant lands—America, China, or Japan—countries whose arsenals could enact a modern Ragnarok upon our command.

CHAPTER 8

In our grand design, a strategy of mythic proportions is requisite—we must arm ourselves with a pantheon of tools, the same that our adversaries might wield against us. We shall delve into the labyrinthine intricacies of legal jargon, ferreting out justifications for verdicts that, to the untrained eye, may appear as audacious as the whims of Zeus yet will be draped in the noble garb of high moral principles meticulously codified. Our directorate shall become the nucleus of civilization's mightiest forces, a bastion of power from which to orchestrate our dominion. It will be a court encircled by sages of the press, seasoned jurists, deft administrators, and diplomats as shrewd as Odysseus, all schooled in our hallowed halls beyond the purview of conventional institutions.

These chosen few will be privy to the arcane secrets of the social fabric, fluent in the diverse dialects of political power, and intimate with the shadowy facets of humanity's nature, understanding every quiver of its pulse. They will be adept in playing upon the psyche of the masses, skilled in manipulating the myriad threads of public sentiment—its strengths, its frailties, its vices, and its virtues.

Our authority's attendants will not be culled from the unsuspecting populace, those accustomed to the struggle of administration without thought of purpose or consequence. These denizens sign away their names without comprehension, driven by avarice or the hollow pursuit of status. Instead, our cadre of administrators will be the cream of the elite, versed in the profound governance games, serving not for gold or grandeur but aligned with our grand vision.

Surrounding our sovereign enterprise will be an elite of economists, for in this age, as in the fabled cities of gold, wealth and knowledge is power. This is why the lore of economic science is the primary mandate taught to the chosen few. A constellation of financiers, moguls, titans of industry, and, above all, billionaires will orbit around us, for in the end, the omnipotent calculus of wealth will dictate the supremacy of our empire.

For an epoch, as we traverse the delicate bridge from present to future, we shall entrust the helm of our state to those whose records create an insurmountable chasm between them and the common horde—figures who, if they dare to stray from our directives, will face oblivion or the stark spectre of retribution. Such measures will ensure that they uphold our interests with the ferocity of Cerberus guarding the gates of the Underworld.

CHAPTER 9

In applying our guiding edicts, one must keenly observe the disposition of the populace within which they operate. A uniform, sweeping imposition of our doctrines will not yield fruit until the social fabric of the community has been meticulously rewoven to align with our vision. Yet, with deliberate and stealthy application, even the most obstinate spirit shall undergo a metamorphosis. Before the passage of a decade, you will witness the transformation of the most resilient characters as we assimilate new multitudes into the fold of those who have already succumbed to our influence.

The very vocabulary of freedom, the lexicon of the liberal ideals – our Masonic herald of "Liberty, Equality, Fraternity" – will, upon our ascension to power, transmute from a battle cry to but a mere echo of utopian dream. They will be reshaped into the mandates of a new age – "The right of liberty, the duty of equality, the ideal of brotherhood." Thus reforged, we shall grasp the very essence of control, for, in truth, we have eradicated all forms of governance save our own, though in the eyes of the law, remnants of the old guard persist.

Any remonstrance raised against us by the world's states is nothing but a ceremonial facade orchestrated at our behest and under our guiding hand. The cries of anti-Semitism serve as a strategic ploy for the orchestration of our less visible kin. This is a refrain familiar in our circles, a subject of our discourse so recurrent that it requires no further exposition.

The Power Elite's New World

In our domain, there are no boundaries to constrict the sweep of our dominion. We dwell within the realm of an omnipotent Super-Government, an entity whose essence defies the conventional parameters of law, one that is aptly encapsulated by the potent and evocative term 'Dictatorship.' With unwavering certainty, I can proclaim that when the decisive moment dawns, we shall rise as the sovereign arbiters of fate. In our hands, we clutch the scales of justice, endowed with the supreme prerogative to both condemn and absolve, to deliver unto death or grant the pardon of life. We are the apex of command, astride the mighty steed of authority, wielding not mere governance but the force of an indomitable will. Our arsenal brims with boundless aspirations, insatiable avarice, implacable retribution, and the myriad forms of enmity and spite.

From us emanates a terror that engulfs all in its path. We command a legion drawn from every creed and philosophy: staunch monarchists, fiery demagogues, ardent socialists, militant communists, and the zealots of every utopian fantasy. Each one, though disparate in belief, is united under our yoke, incessantly chiselling away at the remnants of authority, endeavouring to topple the vestiges of order. Amidst their chaos, all nations writhe; they clamour for calm, prepared to surrender all for the illusion of peace – a peace we will not bestow until they bow to our global sovereignty with deference.

The populace's outcry to settle the tumult of Socialism through international consensus has inadvertently played into our hands. The fracturing into splinter groups has delivered them to us, for to wage war in the political arena demands wealth, and all wealth has merged into our grasp.

We are vigilant against the potential convergence of the enlightened monarchy and the blind vigour of the masses. To forestall this, we have erected a bastion of mutual dread between them. Thus, the unseeing strength of the populace remains our stalwart ally, and we stand as the sole beacon, guiding them towards the ends we cherish.

Occasionally, we must entwine our essence with that of the crowd, maintaining our influence either directly or through our most loyal brethren. When our supremacy is indisputable, we will engage with the public in open discourse, moulding their political perspectives to ensure they align with our objectives.

Who shall scrutinize the teachings dispensed in the secluded village classrooms? The proclamations of a government official or a sovereign's decree may swiftly permeate the entire state, propagated by the relentless murmur of the populace.

In our silent conquest to erode the Public institutions before their time, we have employed subtlety and ingenuity, manipulating the very levers that control their intricate machinery. These mechanisms were once driven by a robust, albeit rigid, sense of order, which we have supplanted with the tumultuous disorder of liberalism. We have infiltrated the administration of justice, the orchestration of elections, the pillars of the press, the sanctity of personal liberty, and most crucially, we have seized the bedrock of education and training, for these are the foundations upon which a liberated existence is constructed.

Dismantling the Pillars of Young Believers

Within the malleable minds of the "Public's" youth, we have sown seeds of deceit, cultivating their beliefs in principles and theories we discern to be fabrications. This silent manipulation has been carried out under the guise of enlightenment, although we are profoundly aware of the falsehoods we propagate. In this way, we have orchestrated a dance of confusion and corruption, subtly guiding the next generation down a path laid with shadows and illusions, leading them away from the truth.

Over the tapestry of existing legal frameworks, without a direct upheaval of their foundations, we have woven a web of grandeur through the subtle contortion of their clauses into a complex array of contradictions. These manipulations have achieved such a state that the original laws, though unaltered in text, now lie obscured behind a veil of interpretation so dense that they escape the comprehension of those who govern. Lost in this labyrinth of legislative distortions, the true intent of the law becomes invisible to those not privy to our designs.

This convolution gave rise to the notion of arbitration as a course, a method where the interpretation becomes the judge over the written word, holding sway over the outcome more so than the statutes themselves.

And should there be whispers of insurrection, of a populace that might rise against us if they were to unravel our schemes before the preordained hour, in the West, we have prepared a countermeasure of such harrowing terror that it quenches even the most fervent spirits. Beneath the very heart of every capital, we have etched a network of shadowy corridors and underground vaults. These subways and underground passages, these clandestine veins of our making, are the groundwork for a future reckoning. At our command, they could turn to catacombs, for they possess the potential to shatter the surface world along with all its towers of power and records of history, leaving nothing but a memory of what once was.

CHAPTER 10

Today, I reiterate a truth we have acknowledged before, casting light on the fact that sovereign entities and their citizens are often mesmerized by the mere facade of political theatre. How could the Public ever decipher the intricate subtext of their governance when their elected custodians are preoccupied with the art of opulent self-indulgence? This observation is pivotal to our stratagem, a subtle instrument in our orchestration of power. As we navigate the nuanced arenas of dominion—be it property rights, habitation, the intricate web of taxation with its concealed barbs, or the elusive impact of legal statutes—such matters must never be unmasked in full view of the masses.

When circumstance forces our hand to broach these subjects, we must not precisely delineate them. Instead, we shall allude to them broadly, ensuring that our acknowledgement of contemporary legal tenets is perceived as nothing more than a passing nod. This deliberate vagueness is our safeguard; it grants us the liberty to selectively embrace or abandon aspects of these principles without drawing the public eye. Naming them outright would be equivalent to binding ourselves to them, a strategic misstep that would rob us of the advantage of stealth and flexibility.

Furthermore, the masses harbour a paradoxical reverence for those who wield the sceptre of political influence. They observe acts of force and deception from their leaders with a blend of disdain and awe, often commenting with a wry smile, "Yes, it is nefarious, but oh, the brilliance of it! It is a deceit, indeed, but executed with such agility, such grandeur! What brazen nerve!" This peculiar admiration for cunning betrays a collective fascination with audacious authority—a phenomenon we are all too ready to exploit.

Chasing the Summit of World Power

Within the hallowed halls where the future is scripted, we plot the genesis of a world order—a tower of power conceived by our design. The essence of this vision lies not solely in the foundations of brick and mortar but in the spirit of unyielding audacity and the indomitable will that animates our vanguard. These chosen few, encouraged by a spirit both fierce and unassailable, will cleave through any obstacle that dares impede our ascent.

In the wake of our seismic power shift, our proclamation will echo across the nations: "Behold the tribulations you have endured—fractured by borders, tormented by divergent coinage, divided by national pride. We have conquered the architects of your agony." Freedom, we will announce, is within your grasp, contingent upon your judgment of our new order—judgment we implore you to reserve until our promises unfold before your very eyes. Then, in a spectacle of collective euphoria, the masses will lift us aloft, a veritable surge of hope and expectation carrying us toward our destiny. Democracy itself, once a tool to cultivate the illusion of choice, will have served its ultimate purpose—to elevate us to supremacy with the illusory consent of the people.

For this illusion to persist, the vote must be cast by every soul, unhindered by the constraints of class or intellect, to fabricate a facade of unanimity—an absolute majority unattainable from the discerning few. With each individual inflated by a delusion of influence, we shall erode the familial bastion and its capacity to cultivate independent thought. The masses, shepherded by our manipulation, will spurn the maverick and heed only those we anoint with the power to reward and command their loyalty. This blind, potent force, a colossus in the darkness, will find direction solely through our guidance.

The architecture of governance must spring forth from a singular, enlightened intellect, lest it be weakened by the division of purpose and the dullness of public debate. For the intricacy of our plan must remain unsullied by the clamour of the many, its potency undiluted by the meddling of minds unversed in the art of covert control. Thus, we must shield our grand design from the scrutiny of the masses and the discord of communal decision-making.

Our stratagem is to uphold the current institutions with a moderate abandon. Instead, we shall subtly recalibrate the mechanisms of society's progression, steering it upon the tracks we have meticulously laid. In time, the institutional gears will align with our grand blueprint, ushering in an era shaped by our unspoken agendas.

Liberalism's Toxic Effect

In every corner of the globe, a myriad of entities parade under varied monikers—Representation, Ministry, Senate, State Council, Legislative and Executive Corps. The intricacies of their interrelations are known to you. Yet, it is imperative to understand that it is not the institutions themselves that wield power but the vital functions they perform. These bastions of governance have apportioned amongst themselves the essential roles of the state—administrative, legislative, executive—much like the organs of a living being, each indispensable to the vitality of the whole. Should one cog in this grand apparatus falter, the entire state suffers malaise, akin to a human body afflicted by disease, teetering on the brink of demise.

When the venom of Liberalism was introduced into the body politic, the complexion of nations was irrevocably altered, trapped by a terminal sickness, septicemia of their sovereign essence. All that remains is a grim vigil for the cessation of their throes, the silent march towards the inevitable end.

The advent of Liberalism begat Constitutional States, usurping the role of what was once the bulwark of public order—Despotism. Yet a Constitution, as history has shown us, becomes nought but an academy of discordance: a forge of misunderstandings, quarrels, fruitless party strife, whimsical factions—a veritable crucible of every element poised to erode the singularity of state purpose. The podium, occupied by those given to rhetoric as much as the press, has shackled the hands of governance, rendering rulers impotent and obsolete, often culminating in their overthrow. In this turbulence, the age of republics found its breath, and from this upheaval, we crafted a new theatre of power—a presidency birthed from the common crowd, a figurehead emerging from our marionettes, our servile instruments. Here lies the keystone of the covert edifice we have constructed beneath the very feet of the populace, or rather, beneath the disparate masses of the Public people.

Behind the Scenes of Presidential Elections

In the looming shadow of the future, a new order is set to rise—one where the mantle of presidents will be cloaked with the gravity of accountability. As time unfurls, we will transcend the need for the traditional masquerade of formalities, empowering our sovereign puppet, who stands answerable for our collective will. What concern is it to us if the clamouring for power dwindles if the scarcity of suitable presidents induces a paralysis that ultimately unravels the tapestry of governance?

Our grand design is such that it thrives on the selection of leaders marked by veiled histories, by secrets enshrouded in the shadows of their pasts—like a hidden 'Panama'—making them the perfect vessels to carry forth our edicts, bound by the chains of their clandestine feelings of shame and the insatiable hunger to maintain the trappings of power, prestige, and prerogatives inherent to their elevated station. The Chamber of Deputies will don the guise of democracy, safeguarding electing presidents. Yet, we shall strip it of its potency to propose legislation, entrusting that formidable power to the president—a marionette dancing on the strings we pull.

Under siege from every conceivable direction, the authority of the president shall be unassailable, fortified by the sovereign right to appeal directly to the voiceless behemoth that is the electorate—a multitude that dances to the tune of our piped piper. In an extraordinary measure, the president will wield the mighty sceptre of war, justified as the ultimate protector of the republican constitution, the guardian of the realm, standing tall as the embodiment of the state.

The hallowed key to the sanctum of legislation will rest securely in our hands, leaving none but us to harness the pulsating current of law-making power.

Furthermore, with the advent of the new republic, the right of scrutiny over government actions will be lifted from the Chamber on the grounds of safeguarding the hallowed secrets of statecraft. The number of representatives will be minimized, tempering the enthusiasm for politics to a mere whisper. Should this whisper threaten to swell into a roar, it will be quelled by the commanding voice of the majority—the same blind majority that is but an extension of our dominion.

The appointments of the Chamber's overseers and the Senate's stewards shall be tethered to the will of the president. The constant drone of parliamentary sessions shall be curtailed, allowing for brief conferences spread across the calendar. As the head of the executive branch, the president shall possess the omnipotence to convene or disband the parliamentary cohort, extending the interludes between their conferences at his discretion. Yet, to ensure that the traces of these actions, inherently at odds with the current legal fabric, do not prematurely fray our meticulously woven plans, we shall cast the onus of accountability upon the upper echelons surrounding the president. They will serve as the sacrificial lambs for decisions mandated by us, a role we envisage for bodies like the Senate or the Council of State, not for lone officials.

The president will stand as the arbiter of laws, bending their interpretations to our whispers, eradicating them upon our signal. He shall propose interim statutes and pioneer novel courses in governance, all under the noble guise of the state's supreme welfare.

Eradicating the Old to Build the New

Through meticulously orchestrated measures, we shall gradually erode, with the stealth of shadow's passage, all established norms and protocols that we initially weave into the very fabric of nations' constitutions. This strategic weaving is but a prelude to the grand vanishing act of constitutions themselves, a sleight of hand preparing the world for the silent and grandiose ushering in of an omnipotent rule that will mark the zenith of our dominion.

Our ascension to an unchallenged despotism may precede the dismantling of constitutional frameworks. That pivotal epoch will dawn when the masses, driven to the brink of exasperation by the orchestrated chaos and the ineptitude of their leaders—a discord sown by our invisible hands—will cry out in unison for a saviour. They will yearn for a monarch of the world, a singular sovereign to dissolve the lines that divide, to extinguish the flames of discord—be they borne of borders, beliefs, or debts—and to bestow upon them the tranquillity and order they so desperately seek.

This collective outcry for deliverance is no spontaneous occurrence but a reaction meticulously induced by agitating the very core of human relations with their governing bodies across the globe. It is a desire birthed from a churning cauldron of strife, a landscape marred by hatred and conflict, a world where even the air is laced with the poison of division. The populace, wrought by the anguish of torture, the pangs of hunger, and the despair of disease, will gaze upon the horizon with eyes clouded by suffering. They will see one salvation: to flee into the embrace of our unassailable sovereignty, which wields the almighty sceptre of wealth and influence.

Should we afford humanity but a moment's respite from this carefully curated bedlam, the sincere wish for our rule may never crystallize. Thus, we must not relent, for the dawn of our reign hinges upon the unbroken night of turmoil.

CHAPTER 11

The State Council shall rise as the monumental embodiment of the sovereign's command, a ceremonial front to the legislative mechanism, serving as the distinguished architects of the sovereign's mandates and laws. It is to become the regal facade of governance, the architects drafting the grand blueprints of rule and order.

Enshrined within the folds of the new constitution is a triptych of governance: Law, Rights, and Justice. These pillars shall be manifested in the form of legislative proposals, decrees from the president cloaked as universal mandates, orders from the Senate, and resolutions from the State Council, all masquerading as ministerial edicts. And should the stars align for an epochal shift—a revolution within the State—these pillars shall adapt to uphold the new order.

As we chart the course of action, our gaze turns to the finer threads of societal fabric: the press's liberty, the right to gather and to believe, the essence of democracy itself. These threads shall either vanish into the mists of history or transform beyond recognition in the shadow of the new constitution. With the advent of this new era, our decrees shall emerge as the singular truth, for any subsequent alteration risks the ire of despair or the whispers of concession, both equally lethal to the sanctity of our infallible dominion.

It is imperative that from the nascent breath of our proclamation, as the world reels from the seismic shock of revolution, gripped by terror and the unknown, they must acknowledge our indomitable strength and boundless might. We shall regard no opposition; we are poised to quell any dissent with unyielding force. With everything desired firmly in our grasp, we shall not entertain the division of power.

Then, in a state of awe and dread, humanity shall avert its gaze, accepting the unfolding tapestry of its destiny, waiting to behold the culmination of this grand design.

Shepherding with a Wolf's Cunning

The populace, in their blissful ignorance, is like a herd of docile sheep to which we, the clandestine wolves, have laid claim. And it is known what fate befalls the sheep when wolves reign in the silence of unguarded moments.

There exists another reason for their willful blindness: we will dangle before them the promise of restoring the freedoms they have surrendered once we have pacified the adversaries of tranquillity and subdued the discordant voices of opposition.

It would be an exercise in futility to speculate on the duration of their wait for the resurgence of liberties promised—a return that dawns in a time that is never to be.

For what purpose have we orchestrated this elaborate ruse, weaving it into the consciousness of the unwitting masses without a chance for them to unravel its true essence? It is to clandestinely grasp that which, through direct means, remains elusive to our dispersed kin. This very strategy has been the cornerstone of our covert fraternity—a masonry veiled in secrecy, its true intent shrouded from the crowds. It beckons into its ornate halls, meant only to cast a veil over the eyes of their kin.

The Divine has bestowed upon us, the Elect, the boon of dispersion—a trait that, to the untrained eye, signifies vulnerability, yet from it springs forth the might that now ushers us to the precipice of dominion over the world.

Much remains to be done to elevate our grand design upon the sturdy foundation we have meticulously laid.

CHAPTER 12

In our lexicon, the term "freedom" is wrought with a complexity that permits multiple interpretations. To us, its essence is crystallized as the privilege to act within the boundaries of the law—a law that at our behest will be sculpted to our desires and requirements, ensuring that all notions of freedom are ultimately clasped within our grasp, for the rules themselves will vanish or birth only that which aligns with our meticulously drafted agenda.

When we consider the role of the press in the current epoch, we observe an instrument that kindles and whips into frenzy the passions that serve our ends or cater to the selfish motives of partisan entities. Its voice, though often hollow, unjust, and deceitful, escapes the true understanding of the populace, who remain unaware of its genuine purpose. We intend to reign in this wild steed of public discourse with a harness of iron-clad restrictions. This will extend to all offspring of the printing press; for what purpose would there be in muting the clamour of newspapers if we were to remain at the mercy of pamphlets and tomes?

The industry of public communication, which currently drains resources due to the imperative of oversight, will be transformed under our dominion into a fount of opulence for the State. A levy, a special stamp tax, and prerequisites of caution-money will be imposed before any press or printing establishment can draw breath; these requisites will act as sentinels for our governance, shielding us from any form of dissent or defamation. Should there arise an audacious soul who dares to challenge us—a feat that will bear the weight of possibility—we shall descend with merciless fines. These impositions, secured by the very deposits we require, will burgeon into a fiscal pillar for the government.

It may be argued that the partisan press would spare no expense for the sake of dissemination, yet upon a second transgression against us, they will be summarily silenced. No individual shall, with impunity, tarnish the sanctity of our government's aura of infallibility. The guise we shall employ to halt any publication will be the contention that it incites the public's mind without due cause or justification. And take heed, for within the fray of those who seem to rise against us will be voices of our own creation, but they will assail only those aspects we have earmarked for modification.

Masters of the Media Narrative

Not a whisper will pierce the ether, nor will a murmur grace the public's ear without passing through the sieve of our omnipotence. Already, this reality weaves into the fabric of today's society as the multitude of news streaks across the globe finds its nexus in a handful of agencies. These agencies, once independent beacons of news, are now but extensions of our will, disseminating narratives that we sculpt with meticulous care.

As of now, we have already entwined our whispers into the collective psyche of the public so thoroughly that they perceive the world through the lens we have delicately placed before them. If, at this juncture, the public's minds are akin to open books to us, devoid of barriers even to the so-called secrets of their governing bodies, envisage our ascendancy when our dominion is universally acknowledged, with our sovereign crowned as the monarch of the entire world.

Revisiting the fate of the printing press, envision a future where each publisher, librarian, or printer will first seek our sanction, a diploma that hangs over them like the sword of Damocles, ready to be revoked at the slightest infraction. Under our aegis, the instrument of thought will no longer roam unfettered but will be harnessed as a tool for enlightenment, orchestrated by our governance. No longer shall the masses wander lost in the illusions of 'progress' and its deceptive promises, which only spawn anarchy and turmoil.

The word 'progress' has been perverted, ushering in a tide of emancipation without boundary or bridle, and every liberal, in essence, if not in action, sows seeds of anarchy. They chase after spectral freedoms, drifting into licentiousness, mistaking unbridled protest as a virtue when, in truth, it is but a harbinger of chaos.

Silencing the Independent Voice

In the realm where the periodical press weaves its narratives, we shall bestow upon each page a tribute in the form of stamp taxes and demand caution money as a sentinel at the gates of publication. Works of brief measure, not extending beyond thirty leaves, shall incur a toll twofold, being deemed pamphlets. This decree serves a dual purpose: to curtail the proliferation of periodicals, those vials of toxic thought, and to coerce scribes into compositions of such length and expense that they shall sit untouched and unread. Yet, what emerges from our quills, meant to shepherd the public consciousness along profitable paths, shall be as affordable as it is eagerly consumed. Such fiscal shackles will rein in the unbridled aspirations of writers, tethering their fortunes to our favour.

And those daring to etch words against us will find themselves devoid of a platform, for any press wishing to broadcast dissent must first seek the nod of authority—a nod we control.

In this manner, we shall foretell any ploy against us and dismantle it with preemptive elucidations.

The written word and the journalistic enterprise stand as pillars of enlightenment and will thus fall under our dominion. By assuming ownership over a swath of the press, we will dilute the poisonous influence of independent publications and command a vast expanse of public thought. Permits for publications shall be sparingly granted, but in secret, we will forge a multitude of voices. To the public, this array will appear diverse and unaligned, but in truth, each outlet will be a cog in our grand design, silencing dissent through the illusion of plurality.

Our arsenal of publications will span the spectrum of political thought—from the nobility to the radicals, even to the anarchists—each designed to play its part as long as the societal structure permits. Like the many-armed Vishnu, our publications will touch upon every thread of public sentiment, subtly guiding them towards our ends. In times of enthusiasm, these outlets will direct the tempo of the public pulse, for the agitated mind is ripe for suggestion and the masses, duped into believing they echo the sentiments of their chosen echo chambers, will reflect ours.

To manoeuvre this intricate web, we shall erect a covert symposium, a central department of the press, where our emissaries, under the guise of literary discourse, will issue the covert edicts and motifs of the moment. Engaging in shallow disputes with the official narratives, our mock battles will merely serve as a stage for our doctrines to be expounded more thoroughly when they benefit our cause.

These orchestrated skirmishes will also fortify a grand illusion—the illusion of unbridled speech. Our subjects will be lulled into a false sense of security, believing in the freedom of expression, while our detractors will appear as nothing more than ineffectual blowhards incapable of mounting any genuine critique against our decrees.

The Age of Printed Deceptions

Within the silent currents of our grand strategy, techniques of invisible influence are woven into the fabric of society, invisible to the watchful public eye yet potent in their certainty. Such stratagems are exquisitely designed to captivate the attention and trust of the masses, aligning them with the shadowy embrace of our governance. By these means, we shall possess the power to stir or soothe the communal consciousness on matters political, to sway and shape perceptions with a tapestry of truths and untruths, facts and their doppelgängers, based on their reception amongst the populace. With delicate prudence, we shall test the waters of public opinion before setting forth, ensuring our victory remains unchallenged, for our adversaries shall find themselves voiceless, stripped of their platforms to declare their convictions fully due to our intricate machinations.

Test volleys of this nature, launched from our unseen third-tier press, shall, when necessary, be swiftly countered by our more visible arms. Even in this present time, one need only observe the French media landscape to discern the clandestine solidarity reminiscent of ancient augurs, bound by a sacred silence. No scribe dares betray the veil of secrecy that shrouds their sources, for each carries a shadowed past, and such scars, once exposed, would strip them of their illusory stature. Thus trapped, they lead the masses who, in their naivety, follow with zeal.

Our schemes stretch beyond the urban heart to the farthest provinces, for it is crucial to kindle there the embers of aspirations and sentiments that, at a moment's notice, could surge upon the capitals. We shall cast these provincial desires as the unadulterated will of the regions, though they spring from our singular source. It is essential that, until we are nestled in absolute power, the public finds themselves trapped by this crafted majority opinion, unable to debate the inevitable for the simple fact that the supposed will of the majority afar has embraced it.

In the delicate transition to the era where our dominion is unveiled, we must allow no whisper of public deceit to mar the pristine facade of the new regime. This nascent order must be perceived as the harbinger of such transcendent justice that even the shadow of criminality vanishes like mist. Acts of wrongdoing shall be confined to the knowledge of their victims and the rare accidental witness, obscured from the collective gaze forever.

CHAPTER 13

The continuous rhythm of daily life demands the silent acquiescence of the public, transforming them into unwitting pawns in our grand design. Our agents, indistinguishable from the laypeople and embedded within our media, are poised to stir the pot of public discourse, championing causes and debates of our choosing. While the uproar crescendos, shrouded by the cacophony of orchestrated chaos, we deftly enact our agendas, presenting them subsequently to the populace as faits accomplis, as advancements too late to overturn. In the wake of these decrees, the ever-whirling press diverts the collective psyche to fresh spectacles, ever-feeding the insatiable hunger for novelty that we have so meticulously cultivated.

Within these new arenas of public spectacle, the unwitting oligarchs, those dilettantes of power and privilege, plunge headlong, oblivious to their lack of understanding of the subjects they so eagerly debate. These political quandaries are realms forbidden to the uninitiated, traversable only by us, the ancient architects of power.

From the intricate interplay of these dynamics, it becomes clear that the public's opinion is but a gear in our elaborate mechanism, a means to smooth the functioning of our plans. Note that it is not for deeds but for strategically released statements that we seek the illusion of consent. Our proclamations resonate with the promise of the common good—a promise entwined with the certainty that we are the benevolent shepherds of humanity's flock.

Pulling the Wool over the Workforce

In an age where the line between myth and machine blurs, the populace, ever susceptible to diversion, is deliberately steered away from the labyrinthine politics which may arouse troublesome inquiry. We proffer new dilemmas, cloaked as political yet rooted in industry, for them to unravel in endless debate. The multitudes, exhausted by their perception of political strife—a perception we have meticulously sculpted— are all too eager to embrace novel vocations, seemingly analogous to their political enthusiasm, yet intricately fashioned by our hand.

To ensure that the masses remain blind to the underlying orchestration of their thoughts and desires, we dazzle them with an array of diversions: entertainment and games that sparkle with the lustre of technological marvels. These spectacles eclipse the grandeur of any mythological pantheon. Our forthcoming stratagem will unfold through the press; we will initiate a cavalcade of competitions in artistry, athleticism, and all conceivable forms of human pursuit. These preoccupations are designed to steer the collective mind away from matters where our interests might be jeopardized. As the public becomes increasingly unaccustomed to independent reflection, their discourse will echo our own, for our voice will whisper the seductive promise of innovation through unsuspected conduits.

The role of the liberals and utopians, those architects of dreams unfettered by reality, will fade into obsolescence upon the dawn of our ascendance. Until that moment arrives, they unwittingly serve our purpose. Their minds are occupied with chimaeras of progress and theories so revolutionary in appearance yet void of substance. We have already succeeded in trapping the collective consciousness with the allure of progression, wherein the term becomes a smokescreen, veiling the truth from all but us, the anointed custodians of divine wisdom.

When our dominion is established, our orators will tackle the colossal enigmas that have sent humanity spiralling into disarray, only to usher in an era of our enlightened governance. And in that time, who would conceive that across the aeons, the threads of countless societies were pulled by us in accordance with a political tapestry of such complexity that it remained undetected through the passage of centuries?

CHAPTER 14

As we ascend to the zenith of our promised empire, it will be imperative that the mosaic of faiths be unified under the singular, divine canopy of our creed. This faith, interwoven with our destiny as the Chosen and inextricably linked to the fates of all under the gaze of the One God, must stand unchallenged. The dissolution of competing beliefs will be a crucible from which a temporary wave of disbelief may rise. Still, this atheism will be but a fleeting shadow, serving as a stark contrast to the generations who will embrace the teachings of Moses. With its pillars deeply rooted in stability and order, this faith will demonstrate its supremacy, subtly binding the world to our guidance.

Our reign will be glorified in contrasts, drawing upon the past's chronicles to illuminate our governance's splendour. The serenity we deliver—forged through the anvil of historical tumult—will be extolled as a testament to the righteousness of our path. Every opportunity will be seized to cast the failings of erstwhile governments in stark relief, painting our regime as the harbinger of a new era of peace, a peace that may bear the weight of obedience but promises liberation from the chaos of past freedoms.

The Public's past errors, those spectres of governance that have wracked humanity with their constant demands and drained the lifeblood of society, will be laid bare, evoking a visceral aversion amongst the masses. They will grow to scorn the notion of such freedoms, which have only served to spawn turmoil under the guise of progress wrought by the hands of misguided usurpers of power. Exhausted by the relentless upheavals of governance to which we had subtly steered them during times of instability, the people will finally surrender to the allure of our dominion. They will choose the promise of new calmness, rejecting the chaotic freedom of the past, and willingly submit to our rule to avoid the suffering they once endured.

Closing the Door on the Divine

In our ascension, we shall not fail to cast a discerning light on the historical follies of the Public's governance, which have wrought nothing but torment across the ages due to their grievous misapprehension of what constitutes the common good. They have been ensnared in fruitless pursuits of utopian social splendours, blind to the reality that their so-called progressive endeavours have invariably catalyzed a deterioration, rather than an amelioration, of the fundamental interactions upon which society is constructed.

The vigour of our doctrine and the potency of our methodology will resonate in the stark juxtaposition they form with the dying vestiges of a once-thriving social fabric, now a carcass of a bygone era. As the new order rises, it will shine like a beacon of hope against the backdrop of decay that defined the former ways of life.

In the sanctums of intellectual discourse, our philosophers will dissect and lay bare the myriad deficiencies of the diverse ideologies that the Public has clung to. Yet, amidst this open examination, our sacred creed will remain unchallenged, veiled in its sanctity, known in its entirety only to our confidants who, bound by their unyielding loyalty, shall never unveil its profundity.

We have sown the seeds of perverse and degenerate literature in the realms deemed progressive and illuminated by the false light of enlightenment. This malaise of the written word, a deliberate cacophony of the senses, shall continue to flourish for a time under our reign. It will serve as a foil to the noble and elevated discourse that shall emanate from our exalted echelons. In stark relief, the deceptions of our articulate emissaries will stand—speeches and programs of unprecedented insight and wisdom crafted by our erudite strategists. These will be the tools we wield to steer the consciousness of the masses, guiding them unerringly toward the convictions and realms of knowledge we have meticulously ordained.

CHAPTER 15

As the dawn of our dominion rises, catalyzed by simultaneous coups d'état that resound in harmony across the globe, a day will come—though it may be as distant as a century's breadth—when our sovereignty is irrefutably established. In that epoch, we shall set our sights on eradicating the shadow of insurrection. With unyielding resolve, we will extinguish, without a shred of mercy, any soul that dares to bear arms against our ascension. The creation of any institution reminiscent of a clandestine brotherhood will be forbidden under pain of death; those secret assemblies that currently exist, which have woven their threads into our tapestry, will be disbanded and their remnants cast out to distant, forsaken shores, far from Europe's hallowed heartland.

Those "Public" Masons who possess knowledge too profound will be uprooted; some may be spared, but they shall live with the spectre of exile perpetually looming over them. We shall decree laws that exile all former affiliates of such enigmatic societies from the sanctum of European civilization, which stands as the pulsating core of our imperium.

The mandates of our governance shall stand irrevocable and absolute. In the realms where we have sown the seeds of discord and dissent, where Protestantism has taken root under our covert cultivation, the only recourse to restore order is through the unforgiving hand of authority. Compassion for the fallen shall not deter us; their sacrifices sanctify the foundation of the utopia to come. The true purpose of a sovereign entity is not solely in the embrace of its prerogatives but in fulfilling its onerous duties. The most steadfast pillar of governance is the aura of power, a halo which can only be attained through the grand display of indomitable strength, an emblem of divine invincibility.

Reflect upon the precedent the ancient Russian autocracy set, once our sole formidable adversary, not discounting the Vatican's reach. Recall the legacy of Sulla in ancient Italy, whose hands, though stained with the blood of his campaigns, never felt the people's wrath. His return, a paragon of bravery and sheer force of will, rendered him sacrosanct. The masses dare not challenge one who enthrals them with the spectacle of his audacity and the unassailable fortress of his intellect.

The Hidden Hand of Secret Societies

In the labyrinthine interlude before our ultimate rise to power, our stratagem is one of contradiction: we shall forge an intricate network of accessible masonic lodges across the globe. Like nodes in an omnipresent web, these lodges will ensnare the influential and those who ascend the public stage, becoming the bedrock of our covert surveillance and spheres of influence. Though seemingly autonomous, each lodge will be woven into a unified system, its strings pulled by the sagacious elders of our order, their identities shrouded in mystery and known only to us. From this clandestine epicentre will emanate the decrees and doctrines that guide the Masonic order.

These lodges will act as the crucible wherein the forces of revolution and liberalization are melded. Comprising members from every social layer, they will form a microcosm of society. Even the most classified political machinations within their walls will unfurl before us, allowing our hands to guide them from inception. The national and international agents of the law, trapped within our ranks, become double-edged swords: at once, the architects of order and the hidden harbingers of our intent, cloaking our manoeuvres and crafting pretexts for public anxiety.

The ranks of these secret assemblies are swelled by the cunning and the ambitious, by those whose livelihoods are carved from wit and opportunism. These individuals will effortlessly dance to the tune we play, the unwitting cogs in the grand machinery of our design. Should the world seem in upheaval, it reflects our machinations to fracture its unity. And should a conspiracy take root, its leader will be none other than one of our most faithful disciples. It is by our hand alone that the currents of masonic activities flow, for we are the cartographers of destiny, holding the map to our predetermined end. In contrast, the Public wades through a fog of ignorance, blind even to the immediate consequences of their actions, entranced by the illusion of autonomy, never grasping that our will sowed the seeds of their thoughts.

Misperceptions of Public Intellect

The masses flock to the lodges driven by curiosity or the tantalizing prospect of feasting upon the lavish spread of public resources, and some are lured by the opportunity to voice their whimsical, unfounded visions before an audience. They crave the intoxicating rush of triumph and adoration, a thirst we quench with prodigious generosity. This largesse is a tool; it inflates their vanity, a condition that subtly steers them towards adopting our doctrines. So wrapped up in the sweet illusion of their own brilliance, they remain blissfully unaware that our hands planted the seeds of their 'original' thoughts. They are convinced of their innate infallibility, never suspecting the possibility of influence, blind to the orchestration of their will.

It is difficult for you to conceive how even the wisest among them can be rendered so remarkably naive when bathed in the glow of their own self-importance. Equally, they can be drained of spirit by the merest hint of failure—by the simple cessation of applause they once basked in, and thus, they become malleably desperate for its return. While our kind remains indifferent to the sirens of success, focusing solely on the fruition of our aims, the Public will gladly abandon any principle to bask in the fleeting warmth of triumph. This flaw in their psyche eases the labour of directing them towards our envisioned future.

These would-be titans, who wear their fierce independence as a badge of honour, in reality, possess the essence of the meek; their convictions as sturdy as houses of cards against the gales of reality. We have nudged them onto the carousel of an ideology, the absorption of self into the monolithic ideal of collectivism. They have yet to understand, and likely never will, that this notion rides roughshod over nature's cardinal rule, which has celebrated the uniqueness of the individual from the dawn of existence.

The staggering depth of their blindness, which we have crafted, is a testament to the underdevelopment of the Public mind compared to our own. This disparity is not merely a mark of our superior intellect but the keystone of our inevitable triumph.

Guiding the Collective Herd

In the intricate tapestry of time, our sagacious forebears, those venerable sages of yore, held a truth close to their seasoned hearts: to reach the zenith of grand ambitions, one must not falter at the prospect of sacrifice nor tally the souls offered upon the altar of progress. Though it has tasted the bitter cup of loss, our lineage now stands upon a pedestal high above the fathomless dreams of the common crowd. The few we have lost are threads plucked from the loom to preserve the integrity of the greater design, ensuring the survival and dominion of our essence upon this terrestrial sphere.

Death, that eternal justice, visits all in due time. Yet, there exists a pearl of wisdom in guiding its hand towards those who would dare to obstruct the flow of our ordained purpose rather than permit it to linger among the architects of this great enterprise. We deliver unto the Masons their fate with such subtlety, such a masterful veil of secrecy, that not even those marked for

the passage into the great unknown harbour the slightest ink-
ling of their appointed destiny. They depart from this realm as if
touched by the indiscriminate hand of disease, leaving no rip-
ples of suspicion, no whispers of dissent. Even among the brotherhood, this knowledge casts a shroud of silence, for none dare
challenge the mechanisms of our resolve.

Under our auspices, the execution of the Public's laws
has dwindled to a mere whisper, their once-vaunted legal institutions now hollow facades, eroded by our liberal insertions.
The judges' verdicts are in matters of gravity, where the roots
of power delve deep. Still, echoes of our will, their perspectives
moulded by our influence's gentle yet inexorable press, orchestrated through unwitting emissaries and echoed in the chambers
of public discourse. Not even the esteemed senators, those para-
gons of governance, stray beyond the embrace of our counsel.

Within this chasm of cognitive prowess, the gulf that
separates the Public mind from our enlightened order, the seal
of our chosen status gleams with indisputable clarity. Our kind
burgeons with a superior essence of humanity, while theirs lan-
guishes in brutish simplicity, their vision clear yet utterly bereft
of foresight, devoid of the spark of creation save for the most
tangible of constructs. This stark divide is not the handiwork of
chance but the intentional design of nature herself, appointing
us as the shepherds and sovereigns of the world stage.

The Expectation of Obedience

As the dawning age of our explicit sovereignty unfolds, when
our benedictions will be unfurled for all to witness, we shall
reforge the anvil upon which laws are shaped. Our edicts shall
be sculpted with the clarity of crystalline streams, unwavering
and lucid, devoid of the esoteric language that beclouds
understanding. They shall be the bedrock upon which an
unshakeable obedience is built, soaring to celestial heights in

their command. From the least to the greatest, each citizen shall stand accountable to the holy seat of power, and this singular alignment shall purge the realm of any misconduct.

This monumental transformation will also streamline the State's administrative arteries, ensuring the lifeblood of governance flows unimpeded. Not a whisper of illegality nor a shadow of power misused will escape the vigilant eyes of justice, for in this new epoch, every infraction shall be met with swift and relentless retribution.

The shimmering halo of our supremacy will necessitate penalties so severe for even the minutest deviation they will resonate with the cold clarity of the stars. Though perhaps a victim of overzealous adjudication, each transgressor will serve as a testament to the holy precepts of authority and law. Our magistrates will understand that mercy is not a public spectacle but an intimate grace reserved for the private theatre of personal affairs.

Our judiciary, confined in service to the vigour of their prime, will not outlast the fifth decade. Youth shall yield a malleable life, while age often clutches to the brittle branches of obsolescence. This policy shall ensure a pliancy to our will and extinguish the flames of communal allegiance amongst peers, tying their fortunes to the mast of our governance.

The young minds ascending to the bench will be indelibly etched with the imperatives of order and the folly of leniency towards societal disruptions. In contrast, the judges of the Public today grant absolution with a prodigal hand, lacking the gravitas of their office, bestowing indulgence as one would cast seeds to the wind, unaware of the harvest they are sowing.

From their example, we shall glean yet another hypothesis for our rule. We will extirpate the tendrils of liberalism from the vital sinews of our government's anatomy, reserving these posts for those forged within our scholastic crucible. And should there be whispers of dissent at the expense of discharging the aged, we shall answer: they will not be forsaken but reassigned to roles befitting their service, and let it be known that all treasures shall reside within our vaults. Thus, our State will never tremble at the prospect of monetary concerns.

The Rise of Ruthlessness

Our dominion shall be etched with the indelible ink of irrefutable logic, each decree flowing as indeed as the digital streams of information coursing through the veins of a global network. Our will shall ascend as the supreme directive, silencing the whispers of dissension and extinguishing the flickers of protest with the unyielding hand of exemplary justice. Like an ancient deity who commands the elements without opposition, our edicts will stand unchallenged, our sovereignty untainted by the concept of error.

The venerable right of cessation, once a principle held by the many, shall be rescinded and claimed by the singular will of our rule. The populace shall refrain from entertaining the fallacy that a judgement can stray from the ordained path we have laid out. Should a judicial mind falter, we shall realign the scales of justice whilst delivering a chastisement so profound as to sear into collective memory the infallibility of our appointed order.

Our governance shall cloak itself in the guise of a patriarchal sentinel, a guardian whose vigilant eyes oversee all aspects of life. Like a father who tends to his brood, our ruler will embody the quintessence of care for the needs and interactions of every subject. This nurturing dominance will foster such devotion that our topics, entangled in the comfort of our guardianship, will elevate the autocrat to a divine stature, celebrating the dictated order as one would a gospel.

Our autocracy shall not merely rest upon the raw assertion of power but will stand upon the solemn pillars of right and duty. The authority to compel obedience shall be viewed not as tyranny but as the paternal mandate of a benevolent overseer, guiding humanity towards a preordained harmony where all existence bows to a higher strength. In this structured cosmos, we shall be the apex of power, the harbinger of the greater good.

Sacrifices shall be deemed necessary, individuals who transgress the natural order shall be uprooted like weeds amongst the wheat. Within the act of punishment blooms the lesson of order, teaching as old as myth itself.

When the anointed King of Elysium places the crown proffered by the continents upon his head, he shall rise not merely as a monarch but as the patriarch of the planet. The sacrifices made at his behest shall be minimal compared to the countless fallen through the ages, lost in the vanity and rivalry of lesser sovereigns.

Our king will not reside in an ivory tower; he will stand amidst his people, delivering orations that will be captured and echoed instantaneously across the breadth of the world. Like a sage whose words ripple out to touch the stars, his speeches will reverberate, carried on the wings of fame to every corner of the earth.

CHAPTER 16

In our pursuit to sculpt a society that echoes only our collective voice, we shall first temper the very crucibles of knowledge – the universities. Within their hallowed walls, a renaissance of thought will be forged. The pillars of this new intellectual order will be the academics and custodians of wisdom, carefully chosen and meticulously versed in the curricula of our clandestine design. Deviation will not be tolerated; not the merest fragment of dissent will be allowed to mar the canvas of their teaching. These sentinels of education will stand not as independent thinkers but as extensions of the government's will, their very livelihoods woven into the fabric of governance.

We shall meticulously excise from the academic narrative any teaching of State Law and any discourse on political matters. These threads will be woven into the tapestry of understanding for only a select few, those whose extraordinary abilities mark them for entry into the inner sanctum of our order. The institutions of higher learning will no longer serve as the breeding grounds for the idealists and architects of fragile democracies, those who churn out delicate plans for governance as if penning a script for the stage.

Behold the folly of allowing the masses to feast on the fruit of political knowledge, which has only served to sow seeds of fanciful utopias and nurture dissent. This era will cease, for upon the advent of our reign, we shall excise such chaotic elements from the educational odyssey. Instead, the youth will rise as the dutiful progeny of the state, their hearts filled with adoration for the harbinger of order, the sovereign entity whose very existence is the bedrock of their tranquillity.

Rewriting the Past

We shall cast aside the veneration of classicism and the chronicling of ancient epochs where folly often outshone wisdom and supplant it with the doctrine of the future. We shall sculpt memory itself, eradicating from the collective consciousness all records of the past that do not serve our narrative, preserving only those fragments that illustrate the shortcomings of the Public's governance. Our curriculum will be the forge upon which the practicalities of life, the sanctity of order, and the tapestry of human relations are meticulously crafted. Education will no longer be a universal right but a sculpted privilege tailored specifically to each individual's societal function and rank.

The trajectory of each life will be meticulously charted, not by personal ambition or whimsy but by the precise role they are to fulfil in the grand design. At the same time, the rare genius may navigate beyond these bounds, opening the floodgates for the untalented is a grave error, thus displacing those rightfully positioned by lineage or occupation. We have witnessed the chaos this breeds among the Public, who have foolishly permitted such absurdities.

The sovereign ruler must not only occupy the throne but also the hearts and intellects of his people. It is imperative that throughout his tenure, the populace is continually educated – in the schools and the agoras – about his visions and virtuous deeds. Our reformation will see the extinction of unrestricted educational freedom. Instead, assemblies in the guise of familial gatherings will serve as the theatre for indoctrination, where so-called free lectures will subtly enshrine the new order of thought into all minds.

Consequently, every aspect of pedagogy shall be engineered to implant ideas that are beneficial to our cause. This indoctrination, already in motion through the method of object lessons – designed to cultivate a populace bereft of critical thought, merely awaiting the presentation of ideas – will ensure the perpetuity of our ideology. As demonstrated in France by our estimable agent Bourgeois, this new paradigm of education through object lessons serves as the prototype for our ultimate aim: the complete annexation of independent thought, heretofore subtly steered into channels favourable to our dominion.

CHAPTER 17

The art of legal advocacy, a discipline that once sculpted minds of logic and precision, has devolved into a bastion for the cold-hearted and ruthless, a cadre of individuals who, draped in the guise of impassive professionalism, too often neglect the noble pursuit of public good. Advocates, with the icy tenacity of mercenaries, have transformed the courtrooms into arenas where victory is pursued with a zeal untethered from the moorings of moral justice, where the letter of the law is wielded as a blade to cleave truth from consequence, irrespective of the societal cost. It is a charade that tarnishes the sanctity of justice, where every minute point of law is exploited, not for the advancement of equity, but for the hollow triumph of absolution.

To quell this descent into moral bankruptcy, we must ensconce the profession within stringent confines, binding it to the world of executive public service. Attorneys shall henceforth be shepherded away from private counsel with clients; they shall operate as conduits for the court alone, dissecting cases through the sterile lens of reportage and documentation. Their voices will rise in the courtroom only after their clients have laid bare the facts under the scrutiny of judicial interrogation.

Their compensation will be severed from the outcome of their advocacy, transforming them into stalwart guardians of jurisprudence, dedicated solely to the scales of justice rather than the weight of gold. As chroniclers of law, their purpose will be reborn, not as brokers of freedom for sale, but as beacons of impartiality. And in this sweeping reform, the insidious commerce that once flourished in the shadows, where the currency of truth was bartered away to the highest bidder, will be defeated. This is the dawning of an age where the defence will be rooted in conviction, not avarice—an era where the once-maligned advocate will be revered as the pillar of an unassailable and equitable judiciary.

The Fall of the Faithful Leaders

In the shadowed corridors of power, the once formidable pillars of the "Public" priesthood have diminished their sanctity, their spiritual mission upon the earth now threadbare against the relentless march of our age. As freedom of conscience unfurls like a standard across all nations, we find ourselves on the precipice of witnessing the final act in the drama of the Christian religion's demise—a spectacle whose concluding curtain would herald an even lesser challenge in our dealings with other faiths, a topic too ripe for the present discussion.

Clericalism, once a force that moved in ascendant tandem with its spiritual progress, shall be encased within bounds so constricting that it will appear to move in reverse, withering under the glare of modernity. And when the hour strikes to dismantle the Papal Court, the silent nudge of an unseen hand will direct the nations' ire toward this once untouchable bastion. As the masses surge in outrage, we shall emerge as unexpected defenders, ostensibly to stanch the flow of blood while ensuring our influence seeps into the very marrow of this institution, only to depart once its vigour is thoroughly sapped.

The monarch of our enlightened echelon will rise, not merely as the figurative sovereign of the world, but as the spiritual patriarch, an echo of the universal pontiff, a harbinger of a new order. Yet, in the interim, as we guide the youth along the path of contemporary, traditional beliefs before ushering them into our spiritual fold, we shall not lay overt hands upon the existing churches. Instead, our assault will come veiled as criticism, a strategic incitement designed to foment division and heresy.

In broad daylight, our contemporary media will perpetually criticize the workings of the state, the incompetence of the "Public," and the fallacies of religion, wielding a mastery of language that only the genuinely chosen of our tribe can exercise to erode any lingering prestige with unyielding precision.

Our dominion will embody the apotheosis of divinity as seen in the deity Vishnu, our myriad hands each controlling a vital sinew of society's vast machinery, omnipresent without the need for overt surveillance. A portion of our citizenry, driven by a sense of duty rather than coercion, will monitor their brethren with the vigilant eye of a volunteer guard, while undue misuse of this civic privilege will be met with a severe and deterring response.

Our network will recruit from all strata, high and low, forming an intricate web that spans from the distracted administrator to the diligent labourer, from those who shape minds with the printed word to those who enact services with humble means. This force, though lacking in conventional power, will be the sinews and eyes of our observation, their reports filtered through the discerning minds of our controllers.

As our brethren now stand compelled to denounce any dissent within their kin, so too will it become a sanctified duty across our global reign, ensuring loyalty and fortitude within our ranks.

Through this meticulously woven tapestry, we will eradicate the plagues of authority abuse, brute force, and corruption—all ailments that our philosophy has ironically nurtured within the "Public." How else could we ferment the conditions necessary for the systemic disorder we artfully manipulate? Among our tools, the most potent is the agent of chaos, poised within the very heart of order to exercise their destructive whims—agents characterized by a potent blend of arrogance, unchecked command, and, above all, voracious greed.

CHAPTER 18

In the twilight of governance, where the fabric of order is delicately woven with the threads of clandestine power, there comes a time when the guardians of authority must tighten their grip on the ligaments of secret defence—a potent elixir that, if mishandled, could be the very venom that seeps into the heart of authority's grandeur. In the event of such necessity, we shall orchestrate an illusion of chaos, a carefully choreographed dance of discord that will echo through the public square, amplified by the voices of eloquent orators. These figures will stand as beacons, drawing to them those enchanted by their rhetoric, giving rise to a symphony of unrest. This spectacle shall serve as a veil, behind which we may conduct meticulous house searches and place under our vigilant gaze those who whisper dissent through the instruments of the Public's own constabulary, unknowingly enacting our will.

Just as the lover of games revels in the pursuit rather than the prize, so too shall we indulge the majority of conspirators. They revel in the thrill of clandestine machinations, their conspiracies a mere shadow play until they manifest into action. We shall refrain from intervention, instead sowing our seeds of surveillance amidst their ranks, observers hidden in plain sight. It is a truth universally acknowledged that the lustre of authority dims with each uncovered conspiracy, revealing not the shimmer of power but the cracks of frailty and the shadows of inequity. The whispers of treason against the Public's figureheads, spurred by the deft hands of our agents—those unwitting pawns intoxicated by the veneer of political idealism—have shamed the illusion of their unassailable stature. By compelling these rulers to trumpet their vulnerabilities through overt acts of secret defence, we pave the way for the erosion of their authority, a crumbling edifice awaiting its end.

Our sovereign shall move among the masses shielded by nothing more than a veneer of the most unremarkable security, for the mere suggestion of a threat to his person would betray a crack in his omnipotence. To acknowledge the spectre of revolt is to concede to vulnerability, an admission we cannot entertain. The Public may dwell in the paranoia of potential insurrection, shrouding their leaders in layers of protection, thereby signing the death warrant of their own influence. On the other hand, we shall not entertain such fears, for to do so would be to acknowledge a hidden truth that could herald the twilight of a ruler and an entire lineage. Our leader's strength will be as the mythic titans of old, impervious and unshaken, a force that stands not behind walls but in the open, defiant and supreme.

Governing with a Fist of Fear

In the seamless facade that our ruler presents to the world, his power will be exercised solely for the prosperity of the populace, never for personal gain or to bolster his dynasty's fortunes. By adhering to this noble masquerade, his dominion will be revered and safeguarded by the people themselves, ascending to a near-divine status as it becomes entwined with the welfare of every citizen. His rule will be the linchpin of societal harmony, the axis around which the orderly life of the community revolves.

The public display of defence is a beacon of frailty within the fortress of his strength. Instead, our leader will walk among his people, seemingly ensconced within a crowd of the curious populace. These figures will form a protective vanguard around him, ostensibly by happenstance, instilling a sense of order and deference in the observing crowd. Such a display will act as a silent command, encouraging restraint amongst all. Should a supplicant emerge, striving to present a petition through the sea of bodies, it shall be accepted by those who stand in the first echelon and visibly passed along until it reaches the sovereign's hands. This ritual will affirm the belief that nothing escapes the ruler's gaze, reinforcing the mythos that his awareness is absolute.

With the institution of overt defences, the mystical aura that shrouds authority dissipates. Given the slightest boldness, individuals feel empowered to challenge the throne, emboldened seditious voices lying in wait for the opportune moment to strike at the heart of power. Our teachings for the Public have been divergent; through this, we discern the folly of their transparent safeguards.

As for the miscreants among us, they will be detained at the merest hint of subversive intent. We will not permit the spectre of the error to grant a reprieve to those who might harbour political malice. In these domains, we shall act with unyielding severity. While leniency might be considered in mundane offences, there is no room for such in the arena of political intrigue, where only the state has the insight to discern the truth—and not all who govern can navigate these treacherous waters with the deft hand of genuine statesmanship.

CHAPTER 19

In our new world, the solitary venture into the political arena is a path we shall never allow the individual to tread. Yet, paradoxically, we shall nurture the seeds of dialogue by welcoming every suggestion, every report, and every petition that whispers of potential enhancement to the welfare of our citizenry. These overtures will serve as windows into the hearts and minds of our subjects, exposing the flaws in their logic or the brilliance in their dreams. To these, we will respond with the grace of implementation or the sagacity of a well-reasoned denial, thereby illuminating the folly in the eyes of the naive.

The uproar of sedition is akin to the trivial barking of a household canine against the might of a celestial behemoth. Governance sculpted with the finesse of public order, rather than the brute force of policing, regards such protests with the detachment of an elephant regarding an irksome pup. A singular demonstration of the disparity in their stature will suffice; the canines will cease their clamour and instead bow in deference at the mere sight of the majestic pachyderm.

To dismantle the glorified stature of heroism that clings to political dissent, we shall cast such acts down into the abyss of ignominy, trialling them alongside theft, murder, and the most depraved of crimes. Public sentiment will then blur the lines between these felonies, smearing all with the same stroke of disdain and contempt. The heroic veneer once donned by political crimes will fade, tainted by the stench of infamy.

We have endeavoured with great diligence, and I hope we have succeeded in ensuring that the Public remains blind to such stratagems against sedition. For this cause, we have employed the press, speeches, and even the subtle indoctrination within the pages of historical academia. These conduits have glorified the martyrdom ascribed to rebels, swelling the ranks of the liberal-minded and leading legions to unknowingly join the herds of our unwitting subjects, as docile as livestock within our grasp.

CHAPTER 20

Today, we ascend to the zenith of our discourse, grappling with the intricate tapestry of our financial doctrine—the keystone and ultimate arbiter of our grand design. This is a domain I have alluded to in whispers and veiled terms, hinting at the profound truth that the arithmetic of governance governs the essence of our endeavours.

As we unfurl the banners of our sovereign reign, our autocratic helm will steer clear of the reefs of heavy taxation upon the populace, for in our guardianship lies a paternal instinct, shielding those under our aegis from fiscal tempests. Yet the gilded tower of statehood demands its tribute, and the coffers must be filled with reasonable care. Thus, we shall conjure the delicate balance between the realm's needs and its people's means.

In our dominion, where the monarch reigns supreme under the grand illusion that all within his domain is an extension of his wand, a path will be carved to lay claim to wealth in all its forms, to steer its flow within the veins of our state. Herein lies the craft of taxation, shrouded in the garb of a progressive levy upon fortunes vast and small. With surgical precision, this tax shall skim the luxury surplus, sparing our citizens' economic lifeblood from undue depletion. The affluent will recognize their charge, their solemn duty to endow a portion of their excess to the state's vaults in exchange for the sanctity and perpetuity of their holdings and the assurance of equitable growth—a growth purged of clandestine avarice.

This revolution of the societal structure must descend from the lofty heights of power, for the hour has matured, and such change is not merely beneficial but essential—a bastion of tranquillity in the turbulent seas of statecraft.

Toppling the Towers of Capital

The imposition of a levy upon the meagre sustenance of the impoverished is akin to sowing seeds of discord and rebellion, a practice that undermines the very foundations of the State, which, in its short-sightedness, forsakes the whale for the sprat. Beyond this principle lies a greater truth: that the diminution of wealth in the hands of capitalists, wealth that in modern times we have meticulously amassed as a bulwark against the might of the public coffers, is a misstep in the intricate dance of economic equilibrium.

A progressive tax, scaling with the mountainous heights of capital, will serve as a fertile delta, far surpassing the meagre streams procured by the conventional tributes on individual wealth. This system currently seeds dissension within the populace, stirring the waters of societal unrest.

The bedrock upon which our sovereign authority shall stand is a balance, an assurance of peace for which it is paramount that the titans of industry contribute a share of their wealth, fueling the great engines of State. The contribution must be tendered by those to whom the weight will be but a feather whose coffers are deep enough to give without falter.

By this design, the embers of resentment smouldering in the impoverished's hearts against the affluent will be extinguished. The wealthy will be seen not as adversaries but as pillars of the State, architects of harmony and prosperity, for it is from their reserves that the means to achieve such a societal zenith are drawn.

Those of the educated echelons upon whom this new tax is levied will not journey through the valleys of financial distress without solace. They will be afforded a transparent account of the tax's voyage, save for the portions allocated to the sustenance of the throne and its administrative limbs.

He who wears the crown will lay no personal claim to the property, for if the State embodies his inheritance, private ownership would strike a discordant note against the communal symphony of state holdings. To possess individually would shatter the sanctity of collective dominion.

Those who share his bloodline, save for his direct heirs sustained by the State's bounty, must either don the mantle of service to the realm or labour to earn their right to property. Royal lineage must not become a parasitic drain upon the nation's treasury.

Transactions—be they purchases, monetary gains, or inheritances—will face the imposition of a progressive stamp tax. Each exchange devoid of this unregistered and clandestine seal will burden the erstwhile proprietor with accruing interest from the instant of its concealment until the moment of its unearthing. Documentation of such transfers will be ceremoniously presented each week at the local treasury, with the names and domiciles of the old and new custodians etched upon them. This ritual will commence beyond a threshold set above the mundane trade of necessities, which will only bear a stamp of tax proportionate to the unit.

One can only marvel at the multitudes of revenue such a system will usher in, eclipsing by leagues the current tributaries that flow into the public coffers.

Engineering Economic Downturns

Much like the ancient repositories of myth, the coffers of the State shall hold a finite treasure, a reserve of wealth from which the machinery of governance draws its sustenance. All wealth that cascades beyond these sacred reserves shall flow back into the veins of society, feeding the great public works that stand as monuments to progress and unity. This flow, this return of currency into the heartbeat of the economy, shall be the crucible from which is forged an unbreakable bond between the labouring masses and the towering skyscrapers of the State and those who sit upon the throne. Among these streams of gold, a portion shall be consecrated as a tribute to the muses of innovation and productivity, rewarding those whose genius propels us forward.

The vaults of the State must never become a mausoleum for idle coin, for currency is the lifeblood of commerce, and its stagnation is as a clot in the arteries of civilization. The issuance of interest-bearing notes has brought upon us this very malaise, a halt in the life-giving circulation of monetary currents, the effects of which have begun to cast a grim shadow upon our lands.

A ledger of truth, an oracle of fiscal clarity, shall be established—a Court of Accounts where the ruler may gaze upon the entire expanse of the State's bounty and its outflow, save for the shroud of the most recent moons which have yet to yield their secrets.

The sovereign alone, the keeper of the realm, stands beyond temptation, for the wealth of the State is his charge, his very essence. With his vigilant gaze, the bleeding of resources and the spectre of wasteful extravagance shall be banished. No longer shall the monarch's hours be squandered on the hollow pageantry of courtly receptions; instead, he shall wield his hours as a wand of oversight and wisdom, undistracted by the sycophants who seek to fragment his authority for their own trivial gains.

The disruptions of an economic crisis that have been conjured within the halls of the Public are born of a deliberate ebb in the flow of currency—a draught of funds creating voids into which states, in their thirst, have stumbled, seeking salvation in the very wells that have run dry, trapping themselves in chains of debt to dormant capital.

The rapacious grasp of capitalism has wrung dry the vitality of the people and, with it, the States themselves. Once the sprawling domain of the many, industry has been usurped into the clutches of the few, leaving a land parched of prosperity in its wake.

The current minting of currency, a chorus disconnected from the symphony of the populace, fails to satisfy the chorus of needs among the toiling masses. The emission of the coin must dance in step with the rhythm of the population's crescendo, where even the newborn is accounted as a bearer of economic personhood. The ledger of currency must be rewritten, a task of momentous import for the world entire.

And let it be known that the gilded standard, once hailed as the keystone of economic stability, has become the harbinger of ruin for those states that clasped it to their breast. The hunger for money was not sated by gold, especially as we have ushered it into the shadows, removing it from the grand circulation stage.

Draining National Treasuries

In the visionary world we architect, the very sinew of our economic might shall be calibrated not by inert metal but by the vitality of human endeavour. We shall unfurl a standard of currency that pulses with the life force of the labourer, its value inscribed in paper or even wood, a nod to the ancient lore and the organic growth of our society. Money shall be issued in a harmonious rhythm with the heartbeat of the populace, flourishing with each new cry of life and diminishing with each solemn departure into the void.

The hands of each administrative sector will meticulously tend the ledgers of this realm, each division a cog in the grand clockwork of state efficiency. Delays in the disbursement of state funds shall be overpowered by the sovereign's decree, etched in time and law, eliminating the favouritism that taints the disbursement of funds and breeds inefficiency.

Income and expenditure shall march side by side, transparent and unified, no longer separated by the shadows that time can cast. This new order of financial stewardship will be heralded with such subtlety that it arouses not fear but acceptance, cloaked in the garb of necessity and enlightened reform. We shall illuminate the chaos sown by the Public's own hand, their labyrinthine financial practices that spiral into darkness and deficit, their budgets a maelstrom of mismanagement, expanding monstrously until their coffers are but hollow echoes.

Our revelations will lay bare the follies that have drained their reserves, leading them to the precipice of insolvency, where they stand, hands outstretched to the shadows we cast, never suspecting that we engineered their desperate plight. The Public's addiction to the opiate of loans, their finances shackled to the whims of foreign capitals, will be revealed as the architects of their downfall. They are haunted by a modern Sword of Damocles, not suspended by a single hair but by the brittle threads of ill-conceived trust in foreign benevolence.

And yet, these strategies, these intricate dances of finance and power, cannot be wielded by us in the daylight. The ironies of statecraft dictate that we must also deny the very measures we propose. Every loan taken is a confession of weakness, an admission that the State has yet to comprehend its dominion. Rulers who should have claimed their due through decisive taxation instead grovel before the bankers, extending the hand of supplication rather than commanding with the fist of sovereignty.

These vampiric loans, these leeches of foreign making, they cling to the Public States with a tenacity that is both repulsive and awe-inspiring. They will not release their hold until they are sated or are forcibly torn away. And yet the Public States, in a display of tragic spectacle, continue to adorn themselves with these parasites, ensuring their own demise through relentless exsanguination, a voluntary surrender to a fate that could have been avoided with the wisdom to refuse the chalice that we presented.

The Stranglehold of Debt

In the gilded age of tomorrow, a loan, especially one drawn from foreign coffers, is akin to a government's issuance of promissory notes adorned with a tax on time—interest. This tribute grows exponentially: in a mere two decades, the state finds itself entrapped, paying a sum equivalent to the initial amount borrowed, and as the years treble, so too does the interest, yet the original debt stands, a monolith to fiscal folly.

It becomes evident that with any form of per capita taxation, the state is no more than a desperate alchemist transmuting the scant copper of its poorest citizens into the gold-laden coffers of foreign benefactors. These coins should have been retained, accumulating like an ancient treasure for the realm's needs, unburdened by the weight of extra interest.

When the loans were contained within the Public's lands, it was a mercurial shift of wealth from the common to the wealthy. Yet, when the tendrils of influence extended, ushering these loans into the external sphere, the vast wealth of nations flowed like a river redirected into our treasuries, turning all of the Public into tributaries in our enormous economic empire.

The kings and ministers, mere marionettes in the grand theatre of statecraft, their superficial grasp on affairs and their greed or ignorance, have bound their nations in chains of debt to our vaults—a feat not achieved without our considerable investment of strategy and capital.

In our dominion, the stagnation of currency will be an anathema. Thus, interest-bearing state papers shall be scarce and minimal, sparing the state from the bloodthirsty leeches that feast upon its vitality. The privilege of issuing such papers will be the sole territory of industrial titans, for whom paying interest is but a trifle against their mountains of profit, while the state finds no gain in borrowing, as it does not engage in profit-making ventures.

Industrial bonds shall be treasures sought by the government itself, transforming from a taxed entity into a wise investor reaping rewards. This shift will uproot the parasitic profiteering and the lethargy that served our ends amongst the Public while they stood independent, but such measures have no place under our reign.

It is a testament to the developing intellect of the Public that they continue to borrow from our coffers, interest accruing, without the realization that these funds, augmented by interest, must ultimately originate from their own reserves—a cycle of financial cannibalism. The simplicity of drawing directly from their own populace eluded them, demonstrating our chosen minds' genius in illuminating the concept of loans as a benefit to their society.

In due course, when we lay bare our ledgers, they shall radiate with the clarity of centuries of meticulous experimentation upon the Public States. These records will serve as a beacon of enlightenment, guiding all to the inherent value of our reforms and signalling the end of the exploitations that forged our dominion over the Public—a necessary cessation within the structured paradise of our making.

Our accounting will be an impenetrable fortress; not even the most inconspicuous functionary nor the sovereign themselves will be able to misappropriate the tiniest fragment of the treasury or redirect it from its sacred purpose. Every coin will have its destiny inscribed in a plan as unalterable as the stars.

Without a committed plan, governance is a journey into oblivion. To march upon an uncertain path with nebulous resources is to court ruin, a fate not even the brave or divine can escape.

The Public rulers, once distracted by the trappings of power and the theatre of governance, merely served as facades for our machinations. Their affairs, managed by favourites whose strings we pulled, placated the shortsighted with hollow promises of future fiscal prudence.

But, alas, these were mere diversions, and the spectre of inquiry into the true nature of these savings—whether from the advent of new levies—never quite materialized among those dazzled by our projections.

Now, bear witness to the consequence of such negligence: the once remarkable industriousness of their people is mired in a quagmire of financial disarray, a tragic ballet of numbers from which our new order will emerge, as pristine and ordered as the cosmos itself.

CHAPTER 21

In our forthcoming era of enlightened dominion, the intricate dance of internal loans will unfold with transparency untainted by the machinations we've exploited under the fading regimes of the Public. No foreign tendrils shall entwine our sovereign wealth, for no exterior force will exist; we shall be the sole architects of our fiscal destiny.

With strategic precision, we have observed the exploitation of administrative avarice and the laxity of rulers, orchestrating our enrichment through the continuous flow of national funds. Our coffers burgeoned, time and again, as we lent to the Public state capital, not out of necessity but design. Who amongst them could replicate such a feat against us? Thus, I shall elucidate solely the workings of internal financial mechanisms.

The proclamation of a loan by a state is a spectacle; it announces the issuance of its own bills, creating a show of accessibility and early bird incentives. The following day, as if by some theatrical sleight of hand, the value of these bills soars, heralding a feigned rush of confidence in the government's paper. The vaults, allegedly brimming beyond capacity, are said to overflow with eager contributions that multiple times surpass the intended loan amount.

Yet, when the curtains fall, an oppressive debt emerges, shackling the state with obligations of interest that only burgeon with each subsequent borrowing. Instead of being assuaged, these obligations are merely clad in the illusory garb of new taxation, a burdensome cloak woven from the fabric of continual financial obligation.

The era of conversions arrives, offering little respite, as they do not quench the thirst of the debt but merely sip at the interest. Such conversions are a delicate masquerade contingent upon the lender's grace. Should all demand their due, the state would stand revealed in its insolvency, a titan bound by its own folly. However, the Public remains blissfully unaware of these intricate financial labyrinths, often choosing the certainty of minor losses over the chimerical allure of new ventures.

In the present, such charades of finance cannot be entertained, for the Public knows our resolve to reclaim our dues, our investments immune to the deception of their past stratagems.

Acknowledged bankruptcy will serve as the clarion call to the nations, starkly illuminating the chasm between the interests of the populace and those who have reigned over them.

I implore you to ponder deeply upon these truths: current internal loans are but temporary, and their near-term repayment schedules a facade hiding the true nature of savings and reserve funds. Left in the hands of the Public's governance, these funds dissolve into the abyss of foreign debt interest, replaced by fleeting securities.

To prevent the loss of the Public's money, these provisional securities are used to stop the bleeding of the treasury. But as we rise to our destined throne, such fiscal artifices, misaligned with our imperial vision, shall be eradicated, leaving no shadow of their existence. The capricious markets of money, too, will be dissolved, their existence incompatible with the stability of our reign. We will not suffer the prestige of our power to be swayed by the mercurial whims of market prices.

In place of such markets shall rise majestic bastions of government credit, whose sole mandate will be to align industrial value with the unwavering gaze of our governance. These formidable entities will possess the might to inject or retract vast sums, ensuring all industrial endeavours become tributaries flowing into our mighty river of influence.

Envision the colossal power that shall be ours when we hold the reins of industry, commanding it with an unchallengeable decree. The world will look upon our financial skyscrapers and see not mere institutions but the very bedrock of civilization itself, unassailable and sovereign.

CHAPTER 22

In the intricate tapestry of our unfolding destiny, we have painted for you the contours of the future, the echoes of the past, and the vibrant dance of the present as it converges into the mighty river of forthcoming grand events. The mosaic of our relationship with the Public intertwined with the intricate strands of our financial stratagems, holds yet a few more threads to be woven.

In the palm of our hands, we clutch the sceptre of modern dominion—gold. With but a whisper, we can summon from our vast reserves any desired amount, demonstrating our unparalleled sovereignty over this earthly realm.

Does not such dominion affirm our divine mandate? Can there be any doubt that with such opulence at our command, we will manifest the grand tapestry that all the perceived transgressions of centuries were but the shadow-play preceding the dawn of true order? Even through force, a new era of benevolence will be established, a testament to our role as the architects of a world restored to harmony.

With golden threads, we shall delineate the illusion of freedom in chaos and contrast it with the true form of liberty—structured, dignified, and interwoven with the fabric of law and order. Our elucidation will demonstrate that freedom is not the constant clamour of dissent nor the rampant proclamation of self-indulgent doctrines but rather the quiet dignity of the individual, honouring the woven pattern of societal rights and responsibilities.

Our singular authority will stand as a beacon of order, the lodestar by which humanity will navigate the tumultuous seas. It will be a source of both power and guidance, steering clear of the cacophony of so-called leaders whose words, though loud and adorned with the guise of principle, are as hollow as the wind.

This authority will be the very embodiment of order, and within that sacred order lies the summation of human contentment. Its halo will evoke a reverence that is almost mystical in nature, a veneration that induces a hushed and reverential awe amongst the nations. True might does not bargain with any notion of right or even with divine edicts. None may approach its sanctified aura to diminish its span by even a hand's breadth.

CHAPTER 23

In the tapestry of the future, a vision unfolds where obedience becomes the cornerstone of a new era, woven with threads of humility and simplicity. The decline of luxury will guide our moral compass. The revival of the artisan's craft will lay the foundation for a society immune to the siren call of unemployment, tethering every soul to the stability of order. Such a society, intimately connected to the rhythm of work and reward, becomes the bedrock of unshakeable authority. In this realm, the intoxicating grasp of drunkenness will be outlawed, a crime against the very essence of humanity, for it reduces the noblest of creatures to mere beasts of burden.

Blind obedience shall only be commanded by a hand that wields power with an autonomy unfelt by its subjects, for within that might, they find the protective sword that shields them from the scourges that plague society. They do not seek the ethereal touch of an angel in their sovereign; they yearn for the tangible might of a ruler, the living embodiment of strength and power.

The sovereign to come, anointed by the divine, is destined to extinguish the flames of anarchy, to quell the inferno birthed from societies crumbling under our subtle orchestration. This chosen guardian must, even if through a crucible of blood and sacrifice, dismantle the chaotic dominions that now reign supreme—dominions fueled by blind instinct rather than enlightened reason, by the primal rather than the profound. These tumultuous forces, currently masquerading under the guise of freedom, have razed the bastions of order to prepare the throne for the King of the enlightened. Yet, their role in this grand design is transient, evaporating the moment He claims His reign. Then, the remnants of rebellion must be purged, leaving a path unmarred by obstruction or fragment.

And in that monumental moment, when the new order rises from the ashes of the old, we shall beckon to the multitudes scattered across the lands: Offer your gratitude to the heavens and bend the knee before the one who bears the divine mark of destiny, a star-led sovereign chosen by the cosmos itself. He, and only He, can liberate us from the chains of turmoil and usher in an epoch of prosperity and peace.

CHAPTER 24

In the intricate dance of destiny, we must now turn our gaze to the enduring foundations of the lineage of King David, grounding it deep within the bedrock of our world. The age-old pillars of conservatism underpin this vital task, held steadfast by the profound wisdom of our venerable elders. These sages, who deftly orchestrate the grand symphony of world affairs, are the very ones who shape the minds of humankind, guiding the currents of thought that flow through generations.

Within the sacred chambers of knowledge, a select lineage from the storied seed of David shall be groomed for sovereignty. Not by the mere chance of birthright, but through the discerning recognition of their inherent excellence, shall they be initiated into the hallowed mysteries of statecraft. They shall be privy to the labyrinthine intricacies of governance yet bound by solemn oath to guard these veiled secrets, understanding that the mantle of leadership is borne only by those versed in the esoteric arts of power.

These chosen scions alone will learn to wield the tools of our grand design, comparing the vast tapestry of historical statecraft with the nuanced strokes of economic and social governance. They shall be imbued with the immutable wisdom of laws etched by nature's own hand, laws which govern the sacred interplay of human bonds.

Should a direct heir, in their teaching, show a preference for levity, tenderness, or any trait that undermines the gravitas of rule, they shall be deemed unfit to ascend the throne, for such characteristics are anathema to the essence of command, posing peril to the sanctity of the crown itself. Only those who can grip the sceptre with unwavering resolve, even when such a grip demands a stern hand, shall be deemed worthy by our scholarly custodians to guide the realm.

By the immutable laws that govern our succession, any monarch touched by the shadow of infirmity or plagued by a faltering will must relinquish their throne to a successor of unassailable strength. The intricate strategies of governance, be they for the unfolding present or the unfathomable future, shall remain shrouded in enigma, veiled even from those who stand within the inner sanctum of counsel.

The King of Powerbrokers

In the forthcoming era, the sovereign alone, alongside the triad of guardians who have pledged their foresight and loyalty to him, will peer into the morrow, discerning the veiled contours of the future. In the monarch's steadfast gaze, the masses will see the embodiment of destiny, its inscrutable paths etched with the arcane symbols of power. His will, a cypher to the world, will brook no opposition, for none may foresee the workings of his imperial strategy nor the desires that fuel his sovereign decrees.

The wellspring of the king's wisdom must be as boundless as the very schema of governance it is destined to encompass. Thus, only after the rigorous scrutiny of his intellect by the sages of yore, the learned elders who have long steered the course of empires, shall he ascend to his rightful dominion.

For the populace to forge a bond of reverence and affection with their ruler, it is imperative that he walks among them, a beacon of unity in the public squares. Through such communion, the dual pillars of society, once cleft asunder by our design, will be united under the aegis of our influence.

The king of the enlightened must reign supreme over his passions, above all, the lures of sensuality, for such primal urges can cloud the clarity of royal thought and judgment, ensnaring the mind in the most base and sensual aspects of existence.

The anchor of civilization, embodied in the supreme sovereign of all, the scion of the sacred lineage of David, must set aside the yearnings of the self, casting away the mantle of personal desire. He must be a paragon of virtue, a figure unblemished and untainted, a lodestar of moral purity for his people. His life, a testament to sacrifice, must reflect the luminescent ideal of service to the greater good, thus upholding the sanctity of his global throne.

AFTERWORD

In the hush that follows the closing of a text so enigmatic and profound, one cannot help but be awash with a sense of timeless intrigue. With its labyrinthine passages and veiled wisdom, the manuscript whispers of a lineage as ancient as King Solomon himself—a monarch renowned for his unparalleled wisdom and uncharted depths of knowledge. The content, so eerily resonant with the present, seems not just a reflection of a bygone era but a testament that has traversed epochs to speak directly to the core of modern society.

The resemblance of the strategies delineated within these ancient pages to the tapestries of contemporary power is not merely coincidental—it feels preordained, etched into the destiny of empires and nations. It beckons one to question: Have the stewards of current realms been guided by the sage precepts of Solomon? Does the foundation of our societal edifice rest upon the principles once conceived in the heart of Jerusalem, within the sacred halls of a king whose wisdom was said to be a gift from the divine?

As the manuscript echoes through the ages, it illuminates the striking similarities between the stratagems of antiquity and the machinations that underpin the corridors of modern power. In our age of digital fortresses and globalized networks, the shadows of Solomon's legacy are evident, casting a long silhouette over the contemporary stage. The ancient script speaks of manipulation and control, yet these are not merely historical footnotes; they are the living, breathing strategies that shape the narratives of today's powers.

Could this manuscript be a fragment of Solomon's collection of esoteric wisdom—a chronicle of power meant for the eyes of future kings and custodians of human destiny? The political chess games, the social alchemy, and the cultivation of public consciousness bear the indelible marks of ancient doctrines, perhaps once housed within the very library of Solomon himself.

This text, therefore, is more than a historical curiosity; it is a bridge between worlds, between the ancient sovereignty of a king thought to be chosen by God and the secular dominions of our contemporary era. The manuscript serves not just as a record of the past but as a beacon, illuminating the shadowy parallels of our times with the sagacity of an era when kings were philosophers and magicians.

In the silence that follows the final word, we are left to contemplate the profound implications of such a heritage. The art of governance, the science of social alchemy, and the craft of the heart and mind resonate within the fabric of today's governance, echoing the profound and possibly divine insight attributed to Solomon.

As we reflect upon the pages that seem to blend the dust of Solomon's time with the digital imprint of our own, we are urged to consider the undiminished relevance of this knowledge. The possibility that the guiding hand behind the thrones of our time might still draw from the ancient well of Solomon's wisdom challenges us to look beyond the surface of modernity to recognize the age-old threads woven into the tapestry of current global affairs.

In this afterword, let us acknowledge the manuscript not as a relic but as a living dialogue with the past, a dialogue that may well hold the keys to understanding the enigmatic dance of power and influence that continues to shape our world. Suppose Solomon's erudition indeed permeates the strategies of the present. In that case, we stand upon a threshold, gazing into a future where the past is not only a prologue but a guiding star.

www.ingramcontent.com/pod-product-compliance
Lightning Source LLC
LaVergne TN
LVHW041224200726
843507LV00013B/2570